The Great
Van Suttart Mystery

By

George Agnew Chamberlain
Author of "The Lantern on the Plow," etc.

WILDSIDE PRESS

The Great Van Suttart Mystery

CHAPTER I

THE NAMING OF MIAD BLAKE

In the year 1870 a son was born to the city of New York under peculiar circumstances and in a peculiar place—peculiar only in a manner of speaking. Everybody knows about the changes that have come to Whitehall, Broadway, Mott Street, Longacre Square, Fifth Avenue, Riverside Drive and the Bronx in the last half century. These spots have grown so fast that they show a stretch of bare leg between the famed knickerbockers of yesteryear and the socks of today. As a result they are so glaringly apparent that when you

[3]

say New York to a New Yorker or an editor of the Omaha Bee or a native son of the Pacific coast, each and every one of them sees nothing but Whitehall, Broadway, Mott Street, Longacre Square, Fifth Avenue, Riverside Drive and the Bronx.

Let me whisper to you. These places are not all of New York—not by a jugful—and in making that statement there is no intention of recalling the peregrinations of O. Henry into the human heart. What is meant is not little journeys of emotion, but common-garden material things, physical things of the consistency, for instance, of bricks and mortar, iron grilles and cobblestones. The next time you think you are in New York get a map or a guide or one of those marvelous truffle-hunter dogs or just follow your own nose until you wind up Cliff to its conjunction with Frankfort Street.

Stand there; look straight ahead and what do you see? A mighty arch, brutal in its dimensions of height, width and depth, abso-

lutely unadorned and yet restful by reason of
two things—strength and simplicity. It was
not made to be looked at; it was made to hold
up Brooklyn Bridge, but that is a mere item.
For our purposes it was erected to frame the
picture beyond it—houses coming toward you
in an obtuse angle and going away from you
into a concave cul-de-sac. The slant to the
right is a narrow alley called Hague Street;
that to the left is barred by a vast gate, a grille
sketched in open ironwork from wall to wall.
Beyond this barrier is a cobbled court of haunt-
ing Old World irregularity, ending in the
blind concave angle.

In this most hidden of the many nooks and
crannies of New York the unknown, welded
to stables and overshadowing warehouses,
stands to this day a dwelling house with face
half averted, so that when it looks straight
ahead it sees the other side of Cobbled Court,
but when it takes a coy glance out of the corner of its eye it can look through the grille,
through the arch and through Cliff Street to

the point where Cliff Street's rounded belly cuts off the view. In a small-windowed second-story front room of this house Miad Blake was born.

There is nothing extraordinary about that. It can be argued that at least five generations before him may have done the same thing in the same place, but the fact remains that Miad was something in the nature of a colossal mistake. Now here is another obtuse angle, hard to navigate unless it is taken with a rush: He was born in wedlock, but his mother was not Mrs. Blake. Look back; look back sixty-two years. Can you conceive of William Anderson Van Suttart falling in love with Mary Malone? His family could not, but he could and did.

With the whole country listening to the roar of Henry Ward Beecher by day and reading Uncle Tom's Cabin by night; with brother getting ready to rend brother and the draft riots spilling blood up and down the streets of his native city, all young Van Suttart could think

THE NAMING OF MIAD BLAKE

of was Mary Malone, her eyes of Irish blue, the black wave of her glossy hair, the entrancing pallor of her cheek and throat. He married her; he was drafted, refused to let his father buy a substitute, and went to war. What his family proceeded to do to Mary was a bucketful of slops on a butterfly's wings.

Mary fluttered to the ground and would have gone under it for all time in a pauper's casket if it had not been for John Blake. The men of her own family gone, she flopped around from one honest expedient to another for four years, and was at the last gasp of endurance when John came upon her, picked her up and carried her to his miserable abode in the house where Miad Blake was yet to be born.

John Blake had a game leg, but he was strong and was employed as porter by the firm of Hendricks, Jacob Hendricks, Van Suttart and Partners. Do not laugh at that name. In that day, even though it is not so far gone, advertising space cost a great deal less than it does now and dignity was worth a lot more. Incidentally, all the Hendrickses had been dead for years, and so had the Partners—save one. Old Van Suttart was practically the whole works, but not all his money could bring his only son William back from the battle-field.

When the war ended and for six months thereafter Mary was all of a tremble; then very slowly, as day after breathless day passed without one word as to the fate of her absent lover husband, the life went out of her, leaving her strong and well, but empty. She ceased to live as far as all individual purposes were concerned, and considered John Blake, his goodness to her, and the amazing patience with which he had slept in a mere coal scuttle of a closet for a year while she had enjoyed the pleasant room that faced upon the court. She married him. Miad Blake was born, and eight months after that event William, her husband, Enoch-Ardened his way back from amnesia to memory and the city of New York.

THE NAMING OF MIAD BLAKE

When John Blake, porter, laid eyes on the gaunt figure of young Van Suttart entering the family counting-house which had never recognized Mary Malone, his rugged face blanched, he reached out a hand for support, and finding none, fell headlong. For a moment they thought he had suffered a stroke, but after five minutes in a chair he seemed sufficiently recovered to go home. He was given the day off at the suggestion of young Van Suttart himself, who seemed to find in this old servitor's emotion a heart-warming token of genuine welcome.

"So you missed me as much as that, John," he said, laying a thin hand for an instant on the older man's shoulder. "Where do you live? I'll have someone see you home."

Upon hearing those words John was profoundly grateful for the fact that so great was his insignificance that no one about the place had ever troubled to find out where he lived. The thought brought strength and steadiness to his shaking limbs. He declined all aid, arose and departed. By the time he stumbled into Cobbled Court he was a changed man. He was not the man who had left it that morning, nor the man who had fallen flat at the sight of William Van Suttart. Like Mary, he had become a shell, strong and well, but empty. He entered the room where she was sitting with the child in her lap, and stood silent by the door until she looked up casually and then suddenly became vibrant to the unusualness of his arrival at that hour.

"Why, John," she said, "what is it? Oh, John, they haven't—you haven't lost your position?"

"William Van Suttart has come back," said John Blake.

There was silence, a long profound silence.

"What did you say?" asked Mary.

"William Van Suttart has come back," repeated John.

She made him say the words once again, then she arose very slowly, laid the baby on the bed, drew erect and turned to look at Blake.

THE NAMING OF MIAD BLAKE

She was a conscientious woman, deeply religious. During all the years of struggle before John had taken her under his meager protection, and indeed until the very day of her marriage to him, she had never been faithless in word or deed to William Van Suttart or her own honor. She was even one of those women who deserve no credit for going straight, so revolting to her nature was the mere thought of irregularity in physical conduct.

Imagine that scene of only fifty-four years ago, when divorce and the scarlet letter were still all but synonymous in the illogical public mind, and when august religious bodies still held solemnly by the damnation of infants. Consider the worse plight of Mary Malone, married through an innate reasonableness to the father of her child after the day of love was over, and now severed from him, without benefit of the courts, by the descending scimitar of fate. For a moment a deadened look drained even the half life of pallor from her cheeks; then, with one of those fundamental reversions that by a paradox rive the dead into the quick, her face broke into the convulsions of a new-found agony of mind and body and she cried out, "What are you doing in here? Leave this room at once—at once!"

For five days John Blake went to and fro as one in a trance, sleeping in odd corners, attending less and less efficiently to his simple duties, and making frequent furtive excursions to Mary's door, where he left small parcels of the things he knew she would need. He was a cut below Mary in everything but the power of understanding. Her origin had been humble, but her race had a long record in self-respect and the things that go with it. She was not a lady; she was basically that more difficult thing, a good woman. John was good too; but he was good only by occasion and affection, not through an inbred overmastering vocation.

On the sixth day as he stood by Mary's door she threw it open and said in the steady voice of all martyrs to conviction at the stake:

THE NAMING OF MIAD BLAKE

"Come in. Take my place with the child and do not leave him. I will come back."

John asked no questions; he obeyed. For three anxious days he waited, rushing out for moments only at a time, to buy this or that necessary trifle. When at last Mary kept her promise to return she found him cadaverous and spent with worry, but his condition left her strangely unaffected. She rushed first to the child, fondled him and examined him minutely to discover the extent of his neglect. The baby was surprisingly well and clean. With the infant caught to her breast she turned to its father.

"Listen," she said as though she were speaking to a chair: "I am William's wife; I have gone back to him. Yesterday I asked him what had become of John Blake, the porter. He was touched at my question. He feels kindly toward you. He said he was greatly worried by your absence and had given orders that you should be found. I begged him to leave the matter to me. I said I would gladly assume the task of seeking you out and providing for your needs if I found you ill. You are a sick man; you must be a sick man. Take to your bed so that I may come daily to—to—"

"—to see the child," John finished for her.

He had taken very quietly the sentence that fell from her lips. He, John Blake, must be ill, bedridden. Well, if Mary asked that of him, that was what he would do. He was not conscious of any special brand of nobility as he made the instant decision; his mind was too taken up with understanding the position in which Mary found herself. It must be remembered that the prejudices of her time were his prejudices. He knew why she had gone back to William; he knew why he himself was looked upon with shrinking, almost with loathing. Mary could live in honor with William for the sake of her child alone; she could not live with its father at any price. He said nothing, but his eyes wandered over her dear face, questioning not her but ways and means.

"William's mother is dead, as you know,"

she said in answer to his look. "His father welcomes me now with open arms, even though it be with a bad will. They—they need me. William will be generous—indulgent. You shall lack for nothing, for I will see to it. All your duty is to look after the child. I shall come daily, unnoticed. I—I will pay you."

Her voice failed her; she broke into sobs, and then John Blake said a strange thing, as though he spoke from a distance, and without using her given name, which had so long fallen easily from his lips: "You have already paid me a thousand times over."

From that day began one of those incredible jugglings of Fate which are forever putting fiction to the blush. Mary not only visited her son almost daily save on the Sabbath but did it without difficulty. The great bridge, in its day the eighth wonder of the world, was in the process of construction. An indescribable disorder surrounded its bastions and it was easy for her to approach Hague Street unremarked, slip through it and around the corner into the haven of the familiar court where she herself was part and parcel of the familiarity and at home.

At the hour of her visit John Blake would hobble into the coal scuttle of a closet he had inhabited for the first year of their life together, and stay there. Something symbolic was attached to this withdrawal. In practicing it he made, without thought of bitterness, an actual return to immolation. He was not divided from Mary; in a way he was closer than ever to her. He was with her. He not only believed in what she was doing; he thought that, being herself, it was the only thing she could do.

Routine is the scythe that cuts the roots of time with a wide swift swath. Do the same thing each day at the same hour, and month falls upon month as a dream that is past; even agony surrenders to a smooth flow.

The baby grew and thrived. When he was two years old his mother apparently deserted him for five weeks, an absence that coincided with the birth of his half sister, Cornelia, unbeknownst either to himself or to John Blake. From that time on, Mary's visits were rarer than theretofore and of shorter duration.

One year, to a day, from the hour of Cornelia's birth, old Van Suttart, William Van Suttart and his wife, Mary, disappeared. It is impossible to give too much emphasis to that bald statement. Think it out. Consider that on the morning of a certain day the Van Suttarts, father and son, were at their places in the family business office just as normally as the desks themselves which had stood, precisely disposed, for sixty years. Consider that Mrs. William Van Suttart came in for a moment, as was her frequent custom, soft of voice, steady in her bearing, and departed in her usual manner. Consider that these three people, all in excellent bodily health, passed from the ken of men during the noon hour of that same day. Not to die in any ordinary manner and proceed to a triple funeral. No. They disappeared—hide, hair and bone. They vanished as instantaneously and completely as the iridescence of a broken bubble.

Why all these breathless paragraphs? Why make a rushing kaleidoscope of the slow heart-beats of so many tragic lives? Why not write the story of Mary or of William or of John or even of the old skinflint, the elder Van Sut-tart himself? Here is the answer: How shall you know the wine unless you know the grape from which it is expressed? This tale is of none of these; it is of Miad Blake. If you would read more of his predecessors on the maternal side, look up the daily papers of the week following their astounding disappear-ance, and learn nothing more than has been stated above. They disappeared.

The name Miad was not synchronous with the advent of Miad himself. For the first year of his life there had been a tacit understanding that he would be called John, after his father, as soon as he was big enough to be called any-thing but Baby. His christening was post-poned from time to time, as is often the case among the poor and friendless, and once the year had crashed to a finish with the return of William Van Suttart, there was no question any more of calling him John, because John was a word that never by any chance slipped from his mother's lips.

He continued to be Baby until Mary's vanishing from the face of the earth.

Soon thereafter John Blake, having become an omnivorous reader of all passages in the Bible dealing with lamentations, invented out of whole cloth and by implication a strange name for his son.

"You shall be called Jeremiad," he said, "for you were born of a tale of sorrow."

CHAPTER II

SON OF THE CITY OF NEW YORK

NOTHING so perky as the three-year-old on whom this terrible appellation was bestowed would endure it for long. Within a month Jeremiad became Miad to all and sundry, and finally to his father also. The child evolved other things toward his personal benefit.

As Mrs. Blake in secluded residence, Mary had been somewhat of a mystery and more of a stuck-up to Cobbled Court. She had kept to herself and her own. As a daily visitant, after the return of William Van Suttart, she had become slightly more human, for it was generally supposed that she had gone out to service—evidently well-paid service—in support of her ailing husband. When she ceased to come, her defection caused surprisingly little remark. John was not so sick as he played, the neighbors said, and so no wonder she had turned from keeping him. As for little Miad—well, nobody needed to worry about him getting along!

With possibly one or two exceptions, no one dreamed of connecting the great Van Suttart mystery with the definite disappearance of Mary from her usual haunt; and in the case of the one or possibly two who surmised a link, it must be remembered that strange things used to and still do happen in New York, and that there are people to whom a dark secret rolled under the tongue is more precious than a heap of dollars in the bank, especially if no method of coining the secret into the dollars comes readily to mind. Cobbled Court bred such persons, as does its vicinity to this day. Go down there, ask a few too curious questions and see where you come out.

But for Miad Blake, from the day he could

toddle, the court held no terrors—none. He went everywhere within a severely restricted area without comprehending that it was restricted. He even entered the heart of the mother of five on the top floor, and that of the hard old man, the proprietor of the building, who appropriated not only the entire ground floor to strange uses but was known to possess the power to disappear through a hole in the wall of the cellar and come out hours later, alive. Miad did not wheedle his way with these people; he attacked them. Was he hungry? He appeared at table without a word. Was he thirsty? He reached for the nearest jug. Was he cold? He took warmth of fire or clothing by assault. His belligerence would have been a nuisance had it not been rib splittingly amazing in one so young.

He thus became the son of the city of New York as he knew it, and this is how he knew it at the age of three: Cobbled Court was the world. The stupendous arch beyond it, cutting a high half circle out of the changing sky, was heaven. Peeking around the jutting corner into Hague Street was to look into the narrow gullet of hell. Of the spindling steel gangway whose construction he had eagerly watched from the slant-eyed window of the room of his birth and which leaped from the fourth story of 81 Cliff Street to an iron-shuttered door of an equal height in the blind face of a warehouse opposite, he thought he had heard much. To him it was nothing less than Brooklyn Bridge, eighth wonder of the world!

No one needed to tell Miad that he should not pass the great ramshackle iron gate that clung to the walls of the constricted entrance to Cobbled Court, barring it ineffectually; it would have been like warning a pre-Columbian against stepping off the edge of the earth. No one told him that Hague Street was hell; he merely gathered that it had a dark name—a very dark name. No one bothered to tell him that the high spidery gangway that leaped across Cliff Street was not Brooklyn Bridge, a monument to the constructive genius of man, because anyone, even a little boy, could look at it and see for himself that it was not.

The name of the landlord, the old man on the ground floor, was Mr. Crabbe; no initials, no letterhead, no bills. Cash passed into his premises for all services rendered; and more rarely—much more rarely—cash passed out. In this way there never was anything in writing, which seemed to suit Mr. Crabbe's indolence or ignorance or perspicacity or all three added together. Let it not be thought, however, that he was lazy or inactive. Quite on the contrary, he was one of the most illicitly industrious and variously occupied individuals in the whole history of Knickerbockerdom.

Mr. Crabbe's premises on the first floor were curious enough, so curious that they defied the mind of man to imagine things more curious beneath. Item: There was a moldering Egyptian mummy, unwrapped but still in its triple coffin. Item: There were the intimate parts of a walrus, unlabeled. Item: There was an indecent stuffed dugong from the Indian Ocean. Item: There were odd bits of ivory of every category—long spirals from the narwhal, curved split scimitars from the hippopotamus, sections and scraps from elephant tusks. Closely allied to the ivory were heaps of bone, some of it freshly scraped. As a background to all these mysteries from near and afar were show cases containing a remarkable collection of mounted birds and strange stuffed animals as diverse as the gamut between a Gila monster and a trachomatous goldfish. In the center of the room was an ancient, much-scarred work-bench of large dimensions, where Crabbe executed orders for sportsmen, for lovers of departed pets, for museums, for fakers—and for others.

Seated on the end of the stalwart bench, which looked as if it had grown into the floor, Miad spent many a rapt hour. One of the remarkable things about him was that in spite of his astonishing belligerence in satisfying his wants of the moment, he was never destructive.

In this regard he seemed endowed from infancy with a full equipment of mature horse sense, so that when he grew restless and climbed down the leg of the bench to wander from object to object and from case to case, Mr. Crabbe did not even feel it necessary to utter a warning, as he would have done to almost any other human being. He understood without words this boy, this tiny increasing bundle of flesh, motives and aspirations; and wonder of wonders, the boy understood him. Because Miad had heard his father, who worked intermittently for the old man, call him Crabbe, *tout simple,* he, too, called him Crabbe.

"Crabbe, will you tell me the mummy again?"

The old man would purse his lips, work a little longer in silence, then lay aside his tweezers or the scalpel he had been using and look at the sturdy child over the steel rims of his thick glasses.

"I'll tell you," he would say, "if it's only for

the sake of your not forgetting the last bit. Listen, son. That mummy there is a tasty trifle, so it is. Spices is in it—and natron, and gums of Araby, and maltha. That's mineral tar, you know, and there's something else— something to make your mouth water."

Here the old man would make a luscious sucking sound with his lips and Miad would cry out "Honey!"

"You're right. Honey; nothing less. But mark me, the honey's been there two thousand years, all of them things has been there two thousand years, the mummy has been there two thousand years. Think o' that; and can you tell me why?"

"Because it knows how to keep its mouth shut," Miad would chant grimly through tightened lips.

"Ha! That's it; that's the boy! Nothing can leak out of it or me nor you as long as we know how to keep our mouths shut. That's the ticket that wins the prize. Keep your mouth shut and your ears open, and nothing won't never leak out of us no more than out o' that mummy."

It was an amazing assortment of people that frequented Crabbe's equally amazing work-room. An occasional savant in search of a single item of information, medical students, with unsalable things for sale, ornithologists, custodians of museums, wholesale jewelers from Maiden Lane, weird foreigners, profes-sional beggars in need of a sore leg, truck drivers, freak showmen and many others less definable went there, not as a certain type haunts the mustier corners of the British Museum or of the New York Library but as persons peculiarly intent on some press-ing matter of business who valued their own time and trusted in Crabbe's discretion. By tacit understanding there came to be only one permissible motive for loitering, and that mo-tive was Miad Blake.

Nothing delighted old man Crabbe more than the attempt of a casual visitor to draw the youngster into some admission of truth or statement of relevant fact. Without betraying himself in any way Crabbe would encourage these efforts by a nod toward the boy or a muttered "Ask him. He knows. I'm busy." Miad was so spontaneously friendly, so self-reliant and assured toward anything that walked in the present or had walked two thousand years or two weeks ago, that strangers were deceived into taking him for an easy mark.

As the realization slowly dawned upon them that here was a hermetically sealed fountain of knowledge in a skin certainly not over four years old, a strange thing would occasionally happen. In reply to some wide-eyed query from the innocent cherub they would tell him some recondite item of research that they would not have sold for a thousand ducats, and immediately thereafter walk away in a daze. It was these rare wide-eyed questions that persuaded them that Miad was a sealed and not an empty vessel. What they did not know and never suspected, so genuine was the child's air of innocence, was that the questions had been shrewdly prepared for the baby lips of Miad by the master mind of Mr. Crabbe. Thus it came about that in after years Mr. Crabbe was wont to state that Miad had been his partner since the age of four.

It was about this period that a huge shadow of a man fell across Miad's existence and lingered so short a time that even the memory of him became a sort of mist hanging midway between fancy and fact. Miad's vague impression was that the giant was a fellow porter who came to see his father, John Blake, on matters of interest to himself. The thing that hung in recollection as an unmistakable reality was that this big man used to take him astraddle of his towering shoulders and ride him down the stairs into Cobbled Court, into the flanking stables and warehouses and, on one gaspingly eventful day, halfway down the gullet of Hague Street, but not back again.

When they were coming down the stairs the stranger would call "Low bridge!" and Miad would lean far over the cavern of the steep descent to save his head from being bumped. That was the part of the ride with an exquisite thrill of danger to it; but out in the court there was another thrill almost as pleasurable. It was to hump oneself up and down on the back of the stalwart neck, hold fast to the shock of wiry hair, hammer with one's heels on the reverberating chest and yell "Giddap! Giddap!" The excursion into Hague Street put a violent stop to this companionship of midget and Colossus, and it happened in the following manner:

When well around the obtuse angle which Miad had never yet ventured to turn, the big man drew up with his back against the blank wall on the north side of the alley, glanced quickly to right and left to see that the coast was clear, and whispered, "Miad, me boy, listen. Tell me now—did your daddy used to call your mother Mary?"

Something happened inside Miad at the manner of the question. He leaned far over

and set his sharp teeth deep in the giant's
underlip. The man groaned and then howled.
He wrenched free, and with one broad hand
under the youngster's stomach so that he
dangled above the ground with arms and legs
hanging straight down, he hit his little behind
such a terrific wallop that the offending teeth
almost shot from their sockets. As it was, the
blow sent Miad sprawling, but he did not cry
out. Had he not known all his short life that
Hague Street was just another name for hell?
He gathered his feet under him and scuttled as
fast as he could scamper for the refuge of
Cobbled Court, followed by a roar of forgiving
laughter. But he saw no more of his big human horse.

Little did the man know of the true inwardness of Miad or he would have reappeared the
following day without a qualm. The boy never
mentioned the incident to his father, and years
passed before he related it in detail to Mr.
Crabbe. The old man laid aside the tool with
which he was working, looked at Miad reflec-

tively, picked up the tool again and presently remarked casually, "You're dreaming. There never was no such a man. Just them dreams of yours."

To which Miad had replied as casually, "I would think you were right if it wasn't that his whiskers tickled."

CHAPTER III

THE PERPETUATION OF JOHN BLAKE

YEARS before this conversation occurred, however, John Blake died. The event made no perceptible difference in Miad's life. He continued as a matter of course not only to occupy the pleasant room in which he was born but to appear at the table of the mother of five when he was hungry and at that of Mr. Crabbe when he was less hungry and too lazy to climb the stairs. Mr. Crabbe had a servant, a drab, inarticulate creature, who was supposed to have food waiting for her employer whenever the necessity for aliment overbalanced the delights of labor and curious research. Not even by a stretch of courtesy could she be called a cook.

To Miad this woman, with whom he was in

constant contact for years, scarcely existed; she had not to his thinking the color or the importance of the stuffed dugong, much less of the Egyptian mummy; and in this valuation he was precociously correct. The woman was an automaton; the very witlessness of her shuffling from one slovenly task to another was what made her valuable to Mr. Crabbe. One would have thought that the death of John Blake when Miad was still in the six-year-old class would have awakened in her some stirring of the latent instinct for maternity, but nothing of the kind happened, perhaps because Miad did not miss his father. The reason he did not miss him was that when he wanted to see him all he had to do was to go down in the cellar and look at him.

In anyone conversant with the laws of the state of New York with regard to the disposal of mortal remains that statement may arouse incredulity; but several contributory circumstances should be held in mind—factors of time, of Cobbled Court and of Mr. Crabbe.

Also, one is apt to attach a morbid significance to the body after the vital essence of the soul has flown, but as a matter of cold logic there is much more justification for shrinking from a mummy two thousand years old than from one two weeks old. To Mr. Crabbe and to Miad there was nothing morbid whatever about the perpetuation of John Blake.

Mr. Crabbe looked upon the quiet demise of the ex-porter within the very walls of his establishment as a godsend. He called in a medical man, secured a written certificate of death from natural causes, and then, with a gruesome memento which the physician had long coveted, bribed him to forget to file the customary notice with the Health Department. At that point in the transaction it cannot be denied that two punishable crimes were committed, but they were so small, as crimes went in the vicinity of Cobbled Court, that one would have required a microscope to discover them.

Armed with the certificate Mr. Crabbe proceeded to expend a thousand dollars' worth of materials, love, skill and professional pride in the embalming of John Blake. That he sought no market for the resulting specimen of an ancient art was just another proof that there are times and natures to which intricate work, well done, is its own sufficient reward. When the expert job was completed John Blake was put in an ancient open-faced mummy case in the cellar and labeled "Awaiting burial." Let the inspectors come. There was the certificate, the label, and any one of half a dozen plausible statements; The body had been forgotten; the heirs were temporarily in straitened circumstances; or, truest of all, the deceased was being held for back rent, long overdue.

At the age of eight years and three months Miad Blake was led around by Mr. Crabbe through Hague Street to the front door of Public School No. 112 and told to go in. Fortunately he was not without the bare rudiments of knowledge; his natural curiosity, aided by his father and Mr. Crabbe, had taught him to distinguish one letter from another and spell his name. It had also enabled him to acquire the very necessary information that five cents added to five cents were the equivalent of a dime in his own experience, and that in the case of Mr. Crabbe five dollars and five dollars made ten dollars.

A whole story could be written about that first day of school, for to all intents and purposes it loomed as big and long as a year. Here it is in dots and dashes: Miad before the principal, establishing, unaided and beyond cavil, his right to public instruction at that particular school. Miad, incongruously clothed but unabashed, before the teacher of the lowest primary grade, declaring his name in a too clear voice. Miad amazed to hear titters from the thirty girls and boys seated behind him. Miad obliged to spell his name while the titters became laughter. Miad whirling, slapping the face of the nearest boy with all the strength of his right arm and immediately turning back to give the teacher his respectful attention.

Miad reproved. Miad asking, wide-eyed, "Oh, have they got a right to laugh at me?"

"No; but——"

Miad interrupting: "Well, then, don't you worry. They won't never laugh at me no more."

In that prophecy he was correct. There had been something so outright and final about the resounding slap that the entire class was sobered. The girls looked at Miad with unconcealed curiosity; the boys examined him with pensive faces and speculated on his weight and reach. When school was dismissed no one bothered him and it was several weeks before his prowess was put to a genuine test. The occasion was an assault on a little girl named Cornelia Van Suttart by Harold Grimble, the best-dressed boy of a higher grade, in a vain effort to implant a kiss.

Individuality in children is that essence which makes them different in spite of and unbeknownst to themselves. Cornelia had it in such subtle form that she almost but never quite escaped notice. She was always dressed unobtrusively in dark material, picked for its wearing qualities rather than for its becoming appearance. The setting tended to dim her peculiar attractions as a shade dims the glow of a night lamp. But the glow was there. Her skin was smooth and of a creamy pallor. Her eyes were of Irish blue, her pigtails had the gloss of a raven's wing and her lips were red and full. In short, she was Mary Malone in chrysalis.

These lips caused the downfall of Harold Grimble in a very real sense. He did not think of Cornelia as pretty or particularly attractive. To his eyes she was shabbily clothed, and her long spindling legs were the joke of the school. Then, too, there was a shadow on her name, something that had happened back in the nebulous past, when she was a baby. He had heard his folks talking about it at home at the time she had first come to school. Her father and mother had gone away and left her, taking all the money.

Something like that. But he forgot these deterrents when he looked at her mouth; it was so sweet, so detached, so kissable. It seemed to have little if anything to do with Cornelia.

He was not a bad boy and it was not calculation but sheer impulse that led him to seize her as she turned a corner and attempt to kiss her. She did not cry out, but the sound of the determined scuffle that ensued was enough to attract the attention of Miad Blake. He turned, came back, slowly at first, and then with a rush. A demon seemed to take possession of him; strangely enough the very same demon that had led him to set his teeth in the lip of the big man in Hague Street. He hurled himself on Cornelia's assailant with such fury that Harold was borne to the ground with a thud. At first the bystanders were highly entertained; then they were awed and finally alarmed. They pulled Miad off of what was left of Harold.

"Gee!" gasped Harold, staring at the imprisoned Miad with wonder and admiration.

Presently his scratched face broke into a grin and he called over his shoulder as he proceeded homeward, "I won't fool with your best girl any more."

It would have worried and puzzled him had he lingered long enough to see how little effect the taunt had on either Miad or the girl. They stood side by side and watched Harold's retreat almost indifferently; then Cornelia turned to examine her champion, asked him for his handkerchief, learned that he had none, fetched out her own and used it to wipe blood from his ear in a matter-of-fact manner.

"It's just a scratch," she said; "nothing like what you gave him."

"I guess he won't pick on you no more," commented Miad, never swerving his eyes from Harold's diminishing figure.

His gaze remained fixed until Cornelia broke it by standing directly before him. They were almost of a size, Miad being exceedingly short for his age, and eye met level eye.

She considered for a moment and then

asked gravely, "Would you like to kiss me?"

"Naw," replied Miad promptly, "didn't I just lick him for it?"

Cornelia frowned, not with annoyance but with mild puzzlement. "That's why I thought perhaps you wanted to," she explained.

They parted without further words, each conscious, nevertheless, of a strange indefinable increase in the warmth of the paling sun. As Miad hurried toward Cobbled Court thoughts of the lost mother of his babyhood kept creeping into mind, for no reason that he could see. Especially did he think of the last time he had seen her. As he passed through Hague Street, which had long since lost all terrors for him, he did not pause at the spot where he had bitten the lip of the big man, but stopped short of it and stared long and thoughtfully at a series of tiny rusted gratings flush with the level of the narrow sidewalk opposite, and lining the wall of an apparently empty house. Suddenly he realized that he had seen those gratings before—from the other side—deep down. Long ago. When he was but a baby. Long ago!

He had been six at the time his father passed from a desultory existence in the second-floor front to a permanent enthronement in the cellar, but it must have been fully three years before that event that Miad had explored the regions beneath Mr. Crabbe's shop. Indeed, he had gone farther than that. He had approached the hole in the wall that occasionally swallowed Mr. Crabbe for hours at a time. He had even——

But first let this hole be described. The bricks, which still lay scattered about, seemed to have tumbled out by chance, revealing a shallow space and beyond it a wall of masonry such as might be constructed to back a flue. On the occasion of this first discovery, Miad had only stepped within the shallow space, crept to the left and perceived that the wall of masonry was but a mask to a pitch-black narrow passage that appeared to lead in the direction of Hague Street.

PERPETUATION OF JOHN BLAKE

That had been enough for one day, but on a subsequent occasion, when Mr. Crabbe had entered the cellar and delayed, Miad toddled down after him and groping along the damp walls with his baby hands had fearlessly traversed the full length of the passage, secure in his faith that he would find Mr. Crabbe at the end of it.

It seemed to him very long, but at last he came out in a series of vaultlike compartments lighted by those tiny iron grilles at the level of the ground above—the same he was now staring at. Here he had made out an indescribable jumble of the sort of things that encumbered the ground floor of the house in Cobbled Court, and finally came upon Mr. Crabbe working at the same sort of bench as that with which Miad was so familiar. He had approached the old man and tugged at his trousers to attract attention to his presence.

He was successful. Mr. Crabbe let out a grunt that from any other man would have been a full-throated yell; he also jumped so

that his erect hair almost touched the vaulted
stone roof. As soon as he perceived Miad,
however, he promptly recovered his accustomed poise, picked him up, placed him on the
bench, nodded his head up and down solemnly
and then gave vent to a chuckle. It was the
first and last time Miad ever heard Mr. Crabbe
chuckle. He looked up inquiringly.

"Baby," said Mr. Crabbe, for the name
Miad was still some months unborn, "did you
come along through the dark alone, or have
you been just behind me all the time?"

"I come alone," said Miad.

"Well," said Mr. Crabbe, throwing a cloth
over the object on which he had been at work,
"now we are going back, and don't you ever
come in here any more."

No sooner were the words out of his mouth
than a flash of belligerence in the child's eyes
made him realize that he had taken the wrong
tack. "I mean, for a long time," he qualified,
and as soon as they had returned to the everyday shop he led Miad to the mummy and dis-

coursed earnestly on the benefits accruing to those who knew how to keep their mouths shut. He also started to tell of the great significance of Cobbled Court before the Civil War as a main station of the Underground Railroad; but realizing almost with a shock that Miad was in fact little more than a baby, he postponed to a later day the peopling of the mysterious passage and the vaults beneath Hague Street with unfamiliar black visages.

What a jumble of records is the life history of any child! Why dodge forward and back from school to walking age, and from walking age to the eventful epoch of toddling? Why jump around like a foolish chicken on a hot stove? Why not set down the narrative of Miad Blake in sane chronological order—diapers to kilts, kilts to smock, smock to pants, and pants to trousers? Because that is not the way Miad grew, nor is it the way any child grows.

Things as they happen are seldom perceived at the apparent moment of occurrence. A brick falling on one's head from six stories up is not an event; it is a termination. But a tossed pebble, or a slowly settling stone may develop in its own time into an event of enormous proportions—today, nothing; yesterday, an avalanche. Read that again. Remember it.

Miad was not an obedient child; though he was not destructive there was but one method of insuring that he would do a thing, and that was to tell him not to do it. Having discovered, as sooner or later he discovered all things, the hiding place where Mr. Crabbe kept the huge key to the shop during his frequent absences, Miad said nothing and waited for the necessary increase of a half inch in stature that enabled him to reach the keyhole and unlock the door. He was told peremptorily by both Mr. Crabbe and his father never to do so again, and, true to form, he proceeded to disobey whenever the chances appeared to be against detection.

On one such occasion he had no sooner penetrated well into the deserted shop than his mother appeared in the doorway. His regard for her was quite different from his attitude toward his father or any other human being. To be caught by her in wrongdoing struck panic to his sturdy heart. Without pausing to reason he had turned and rushed for the stairway at the back of the room, cackling with nervous laughter as he went. She cried out "Baby!" twice; then followed him with such speed that she was just in time to catch the flick of his kilt as it disappeared through the hole in the wall of the cellar. From there on, perforce, she followed more slowly, feeling her way, and struck silent by wonder.

The child issued from the dark passage well in the lead, and, hearing her approach, passed from one vaultlike chamber to another until he reached the next to the last of the series. Here he paused, tottered and almost tumbled with surprise, for the last chamber of all was forevermore inaccessible, the arch which once gave upon it barred by a mass of débris. Even the one in which he stood was strangely changed and glorified. It was not dimly illumined by the tiny grilles as he had remembered it; it was bright as day.

He stopped, spellbound, and there she came upon him, standing with his hands fixed in an open gesture of amazement within the aureole of a slanting bar of golden light. At his feet was the large stone which, rolling from a breach in the roof of the second chamber, had let in the sunlight that was dazzling his uplifted eyes. She had passed that spot in the street only five minutes before, and had glanced curiously at the hole in the ground and at the departing workmen who had just caused it in the process of leveling and refilling indentations along the line of the bridge.

Remember that too; the street, the hole, the workmen gone for their nooning to some public house.

But now she had no thought for external things. She ran forward, sank upon the stone, swept the child into her straining arms and cried out, "Oh, baby,—my dear, dear boy, why did you run from your mother?"

The boy's tense body did not yield; if anything it stiffened. A deep shadow had suddenly dimmed the sunlight and darkened his illumined face. A voice from without—from up in the street—spoke, its tones magnified by the funnel-like opening, but still hard and thin as the edge of a saw: "Ha! What did I tell you, William? A bit of fortune; or perhaps it was the finger of God that pierced this hole."

For an instant Mary, his mother, had remained quite still. Still as the stone she sat upon. Even her soft breast and the throbbing of her heart became as stone. The pallor of her face faded to white. White like milk. Whiter than milk. Like paper. Then she had turned her head with a slow upward movement and gulped, "William! Mr. Van—"

Miad remembered little more; only her cry with a note of panic in it as all the light was suddenly blotted out and pebbles and earth began to trickle down into the chamber: "Run, darling! Run!"

She had given him a quick thrust, and he had run, the note of panic in her voice thrilling through his scampering little legs. Something was after him, something big, something that followed with a roar and stopped with a dull thud. An avalanche—an avalanche of caving stones and mortar; and yet, in that day and at that time, to the baby Miad it was nothing more than a pursuing sound! He had bruised his hands and even his face in the dark passage, but once safe upon the cellar stairs he stopped, listened, waited, his eyes fixed on the ragged hole in the brick wall. His mother did not come; no one came. Presently he crept up to the shop and out of it. It seemed impossible that Mr. Crabbe had not returned, for children do not measure time by minutes and seconds. He had locked the door and restored the key to its hiding place.

How tiny a boy; how great an event!

PERPETUATION OF JOHN BLAKE

Stupendous! How near together; how far apart!

Had the elder Van Suttart been suspicious of the comings and goings of his son's wife for long? Was it chance that had shown her to father and son as she hurried along the torn bit of Hague Street to her tryst? Following upon her footsteps, had they come upon the hole and looked down it just as she had done swift moments before?

"Ha! What did I tell you, William? A bit of fortune; or perhaps it was the finger of God that pierced this hole!"

Terrible voice, cold as chisel steel. Portentous words, turning a woman's soft breast and throbbing heart to stone. Poor Mary Malone! More agony? Incredible! More torture coming to her hard-pressed soul? Despair. But wait. The true finger of a merciful God, pushing pebbles, pushing earth. Premonition. "Run, darling! Run!" The rumble and roar. The avalanche. Silence. The returning laborers, pleased to find their work done for them. No sign of the threefold tomb. Not one.

Miad Blake, grown from that day to eight years and five months old, and fresh from his battle for Cornelia, stood in Hague Street staring at the tiny rusted iron grilles which twice he had seen from their other side and then raised his eyes slowly to the beetling masonry of the bastions of Brooklyn Bridge. It was upon that very towering wall he had gazed through the amazing hole in the roof of the underground chamber. Suddenly he remembered with a strange constriction of the throat that his mother had not reproached him after all! No. She had held him close and spoken not with anger but with love in her voice: "Oh, baby, my dear, dear boy, why did you run from your mother?" And then, deep from within her, her eyes wide, compelling, "Run, darling! Run!" He wondered why she had never come again. He had never heard of the great Van Suttart mystery.

CHAPTER IV

WHEN Miad was eleven and Cornelia Van
Suttart just two years younger, he called her
Corny for the first time in their long acquain-
tanceship. Up to that day it simply had not
occurred to him to call her by her nickname.
It happened in the most casual manner. At
the corner of Roosevelt and the New Bowery,
just as she was about to turn north on her
homeward way from school, and he south, he
said, "So long, Corny."

Her slight figure drew erect and quivering.
Her eyes blazed; her lips trembled and twist-
ed. "Oh!" she cried as if he had struck her.
"Oh!"

Miad stared at her in dumfounded amazement. "Say," he demanded, "what's the matter with you?"

[55]

"You—you called me Corny!" gulped Cornelia, and burst into tears.

Miad, whose basic principle was action, and who when in doubt invariable resorted to his fists, stood before her, numb, paralyzed, and watched her weep. For once in his life he knew not what to do, and did it. He neither spoke nor moved. To all intents and purposes he was dead in his frayed pants and worn-out shoes. Still weeping, Cornelia turned from him and resumed her way, her head bowed, her thin shoulders shaking to her sobs. And speaking of thin shoulders, those were the days of the tightest sleeves and the most bebuttoned, skinny little jackets of all time.

Miad came to life slowly. No mortal was less introspective than himself, but even at his tender age he had often been forced to the expert deduction by which thrives all that division of humanity which lives on its wits. He perceived that Cornelia disliked her nickname of Corny, probably because of its unfortunate connotation with corns. He realized vaguely that her innate delicacy shrank from the superficial affinity between the two sounds and promptly resolved that henceforth neither himself nor anyone else should call her Corny.

He wandered home with staring, unseeing eyes, pondering purposefully on just how he would issue the edict on the following day. Owing to this foresight the matter of the decree progressed normally. The first time a boy chanted "Corny, Corny, Corny! Do you love me? No sir-ree!" his song stopped short in the middle of a bar as his eyes fell on the sturdy figure of Miad Blake planted directly before him in a well-known attitude of belligerence.

"She don't like to be called Corny," said Miad with deceptive mildness, "and nobody ain't going to do it no more."

The boy eyed him for a moment with astonishment and then realized that it was fight or crawl. "Aw, gee!" he muttered. "I don't want to call her Corny. I don't care what I call her, and I guess nobody else cares neither, only her and you."

Cornelia had thick eyelashes which ordinarily veiled her eyes, and a mouth that was rather wide though full, but which curled up sensitively at the corners. Miad caught a fleeting-glance of gratitude and a trembling of one of the turned-up corners of her lips, and gathered that he was on his way to forgiveness for his offense of the previous day, but something elemental within him told him that this was not enough.

With any other girl the amends would have been more than sufficient, but somehow Cornelia was different. To hurt her was especially wrong. He did not know why, but it was all wrong, like—well—like striking one's own mother.

Now all men, eighty years old or ten years young, are cast in the same mold when it comes to wounding the woman who for any reason is nearest to their heart. At such times a cry goes up which is universal, though

single to each instance. "What can I give her
to make it right? What treasured possession
can I share with her? What sacrificial offering can I lay upon the altar of atonement?"

Consider that Miad's apparel was a source
of strictly silent wonder to all with whom he
came in contact outside the periphery of Vandewater and Frankfort Streets, not because
of its perpetual ill fit but by reason of its
astonishing variety. Just to illustrate, let it
be recorded that at the age of eight he went
into long trousers—very long trousers—and
at ten had returned to knee pants. No other
boy could have weathered such an ordeal, but
to Miad it was all in the day's run of luck.
What he could pick up in Cobbled Court or
what was handed him absent-mindedly by his
weird patron, Mr. Crabbe, was what he wore;
and it should be remembered that the more
ludicrous the result to the outside world, the
more did it harmonize with Cobbled Court.

To look at his unbrushed hair erupting from
a broken crowned hat, at his disintegrating

garments and unwashed hands, and then to take in with a glance Cornelia's air of refinement, which triumphed over the scant simplicity of her clothing, was to conclude instanter that there was nothing on earth that Miad could give her in spite of the purposeful fire in his eyes which made them seem to protrude in their effort to meet the world at large ninetenths of the way. But listen to this:

Had anyone told Miad that the locale of his birth was unique in the annals of the New World and assured him that it surpassed in every essential particular the bandit dens made vivid in the Forty Thieves, Robin Hood, Lorna Doone, Robbery Under Arms, and even the storied haunts of Captain Kidd, he would have grunted, "Ya! Go on!" But deep in his heart he would have known the saying for the truth. What he could not have believed was that anyone else could fully appreciate the peculiar characteristics of Cobbled Court—always excepting old man Crabbe.

Also if Mr. Crabbe had built the location for

his strange business and then arranged the city of New York around it according to his individual fancy the result could not have been better adapted to his purposes. Here are the facts: Imagine one-third of a pumpkin pie; hold with the corner toward you; run your tongue straight in, work it around a bit and draw it out. The hole your tongue leaves is Cobbled Court; the hundred and twenty degrees of crust rim is Vandewater Street, swinging around from Frankfort into Pearl to within forty yards of Hague. The clean cut to your right is Hague Street itself; the one to the left is Brooklyn Bridge, roofing a high alley under its northern edge, dark by day and pitch black by night, and barred at each end by iron gates bearing the sign, "Open to the public from 8 A.M. to 6 P.M."

To a casual observer Cobbled Court looked —and still looks, for that matter—like a genuine cul-de-sac. Glancing at it through the ramshackle iron gate and the great arch which faces the end of Cliff Street one would have said that there was only a single way in and the same way out; but for Miad the possibilities of entrance and exit were so various that they defied surveillance. He could walk in frankly through the arch or come through the narrow, straight gullet of Hague Street from the east or through the cavernous alley under the northern eaves of the bridge, which alley was an innovation to his seniors but not to Miad, for he and it were coeval. To him it was as old as time itself.

Nor was this all. Years ago he had learned that he could saunter around the curve of Vandewater from either end, stop halfway at the entrance to Maclintock's Warehouse, Importers of Hides, Green and Cured, loiter on the two broad shallow steps of wood, enter, meander among the odorous bales, pass through a narrow musty corridor into Maclintock's dray-horse stables, and encounter his own front door, staring him in the face with a suddenness and propinquity to which he never grew wholly accustomed.

COBBLED COURT, MYSTIC MAZE

Add to all these, the most mysterious exit of all, the underground passage leading off from the cellar of Crabbe's shop in Cobbled Court in the direction of Hague Street. Where did it really end? Was it an exit or merely a well laid on its side? Miad did not know—not definitely. He only knew that the clammy tunnel debouched in a series of vaulted chambers.

The advantages to Mr. Crabbe of so hidden and yet ubiquitous a situation as Cobbled Court will develop in due course, but the profit to Miad is immediately apparent. At the moment when the children of the primary class as a unanimous body had laughed at his name on the crucial occasion of his first day at school, he had perceived that between himself and these a great gulf was fixed. It went almost without saying that he would not permit them to laugh at him again; his perky nature, two hard little fists, chunky build and, above all, his amazingly belligerent eyes had seen to that.

But above and beyond the just returns of prowess, he had absorbed more or less instinctively the determination to preserve the isolation in private life which was his only birthright. None of his playmates knew where he lived and he made up his mind that none was ever to find out, at least not by sleuthing. Thus Cobbled Court took on more and more the aspects of a personal possession.

It is true that on the top floor of the building in which he resided lived the mother of five and her offspring, but, as it happened, this brood was all older than Miad by the huge minimum of three years and in its entirety went to work and not to school. As a result Miad was the only scholar recruited from Cobbled Court and its immediate environs.

Another feature had strengthened his resolve to play only in other people's back yards to the complete exclusion of his own, and that was the peculiar conformation of New York as he had grown to know it at this period of his life.

On East Broadway still lingered a few stately residences reminiscent of its day of fashion, and the same was true of Madison Street—not Madison Avenue by three miles and as many decades—and it was from these streets that the enrollment of Number 112 was largely drawn. It was natural that Miad should defend the stable-like attributes of Cobbled Court from the snobbish inspection of his more stylish schoolfellows.

Nevertheless let it not be thought that he was an ugly duckling among prigs, for nothing could be further from the truth. Away from the benignly grim atmosphere of Cobbled Court he was a youngster among youngsters, warmly regarded by many, respected by all, welcomed by shouts of "Hi! Miad!" whenever there was a bout of miggles or three-o'-cat in the empty lot on New Chambers Street or a game of cross tag amid the jumble of short blocks and sharp corners which marked the intersections and interstices of Oak, Chestnut, Pearl, Cherry, Roosevelt and Madison Streets. Incidentally and as befitted his age, he had no use for girls. He did not actively disdain them; he merely felt crucified to his outlandish garb when they were around.

As regards the female sex, however, Cornelia Van Suttart formed a small but towering exception. Toward this slip of a girl, so quiet in her dress and ways, petal white as to cheeks, dangling pigtails lustrous with the gloss of a raven's wing and possessed of hidden deep blue eyes, Miad felt no instinctive reticence whatever, nor did she toward him. By no means was he drawn by the eyes, hair and complexion listed above. They did not enter into his consciousness; he did not even know that she had them. All he knew was that she was Cornelia; all she knew was that he was Miad and that it came easy to stand shoulder to shoulder whenever they felt like it.

So supremely natural was this allegiance that it actually precluded gibes from their playmates. Just as it never entered Miad Blake's head to caress Cornelia Van Suttart or use a tone of tenderness toward her any more than toward any other mortal, so it never occurred to their schoolfellows, hawk-eyed only for the offal of sentimental mush, to question so matter-of-fact a friendship.

However, if the one living human being out of the millions which comprised the city of New York who suspected the truth, had told Miad and Cornelia that Mary Malone, Mary Van Suttart and Mary Blake were three names for one person, making Cornelia half sister to Miad, Cornelia's eyes would have grown wide open, profoundly luminous, ineffably soft, and Miad would have fallen over dead with the shock.

CHAPTER V

FORTUNATELY for the continuance of this story, one individual out of an odd number of millions is not easily stumbled upon, and the man who suspected the truth was so wraith-like a memory of Miad's babyhood that, had he appeared, Miad would almost indubitably have taken him for a phantom and run, as is the privilege of the bravest when confronted with the supernatural. Fate might yet draw the long bow of coincidence and shoot its single arrow to the mark so swiftly that the shaft could not be dodged, but in the meantime enough has been said to show that Miad was by no means destitute of treasures, abstract but most real, to be shared with a trusted play-mate.

MIAD SHARES HIS TREASURE

"Cornelia," he said on a happy day when a sudden colic incapacitated the teacher of their last class of the afternoon, "you ain't got to go home yet. Listen. Can you keep a secret?"

At the magic word her eyes flashed wide open for an instant. "A secret, Miad?" she whispered.

"Sure," said Miad. "An honest-to-goodness secret. You don't have to cross your heart nor nothing like that. That's kids' stuff. Old man Crabbe says the reason a mummy lasts two thousand years is because it knows how to keep its mouth shut, and if you can keep your mouth shut for two thousand years I guess maybe I can show you something I wouldn't show anyone else."

"I can, Miad," said Cornelia earnestly. "I can keep a secret forever, and that's more than two thousand years even. Where is it?"

"You come with me," said Miad.

He led her across the New Bowery into Pearl to give the other children time to go their ways, and then doubled back toward

Vandewater. The mere act of initiating Cornelia into the labyrinth of Cobbled Court con-
stituted in itself a great boon, but Miad was
not old enough to conceive of it as such. While
subconsciously the responsibility involved
weighed heavily upon him, his youthful imagination demanded a more definite offering as
the supreme gift with which he was to make
atonement for having wounded Cornelia, and
he had finally settled upon a strange object.
He would share with her nothing less than the
contemplative enjoyment of his embalmed
father, John Blake.

At the corner of Pearl and Vandewater,
Miad halted, as was his custom, to satisfy himself that the coast was clear of acquaintances,
and then plunged into the long curve of the
latter street. When the strangely assorted
pair of children entered Maclintock's encumbered warehouse nobody paid the slightest
attention to them, which gave Cornelia courage to seize Miad's hand and follow him
through the dark and musty corridor that led

them into the stables. They had only a few steps to go to attain to the refuge of Cobbled Court, but the broad doorway of the stable made it as light as the passage had been gloomy.

"Hey! Miad!" called the mucker-out on duty. "Got a girl! Eh, Miad? Look out she don't step quick and break one of them pipe-stem legs. Eh, Miad?"

"She ain't a girl," muttered Miad, never swerving his gaze. "She's just Cornelia."

Being no fool he realized that there were a few large men he could not thrash at present, but he registered a black mark against the stable attendant for future attention. He also dropped Cornelia's hand very suddenly. Thirty seconds later they entered Crabbe's shop and came face to face with the old man himself. For a moment Cornelia looked at him and he looked at Cornelia. She saw a tall bent figure which looked like a twisted strip of raw-hide fitted with a white-haired head and glasses over whose steel rims two deeply set gray eyes

twinkled like the shiny points of a pair of gim-
lets. What Crabbe saw was an immature
specimen of a sex for which he had little
use.

"Got a girl. Eh, Miad?" said Mr. Crabbe.

"She ain't a girl," repeated Miad doggedly.
"She's just Cornelia, and she says she can
keep her mouth shut forever, and I guess that's
a lot longer than two thousand years even."

"I reckon it is," said the old man, pinching
his under lip pensively, "but I doubt she could
do it unless we should stuff her with honey
like we done your dad."

Cornelia said primly that she was not allowed to eat away from home. Miad blushed
and Mr. Crabbe grinned, but Cornelia saw
neither blush nor grin. Her eyes had passed
Mr. Crabbe and promptly she followed them,
moving cautiously at first with one hand on the
long work-bench, and then stepping lightly
from one astonishing wonder to another.

Before the stuffed dugong, before a side
table upon which were scattered numerous

dull-covered but exotic-looking journals, before a rare specimen of the newly discovered gorilla, before jars of pickled snakes, cases of butterflies, the Gila monster, the trachomatous goldfish and, finally, before the Egyptian mummy, she poised on one foot to emit her ecstatic little cry of "Oh, Miad!"

"You wait," said Miad, following her around. "You come with me."

He guided her at last down the cellar stairway at the rear of the shop, warning her to look where she was going, for Cornelia's head was swiveled on her shoulders in the traditional position so disastrous to Lot's wife. Never in her restricted life had her hidden eyes stayed open so wide and so long. She followed Miad with the resigned air of a woman abandoning fascinating shop windows to accompany her man to a masculine ball game. But once she found herself in the cellar, its shadowy mysteries seized her entire attention with a suddenness that made her catch her breath. To add to her excitement Miad took her by the wrist, and immediately she became conscious of an unaccustomed tensity in his bearing.

"Look," he said.

In the soft glow of light shed by a shallow, dust-begrimed window reposed the placid effigy of John Blake; nay, John Blake himself. The Egyptian mummy case into which he was neatly fitted was propped higher at the head than at the foot, but both trestles were so low that even the diminutive Cornelia could get an uninterrupted view. Never had she seen anything more real, more approachable and, in a manner of speaking, more companionable. The long white mustache and curling beard looked as if the faintest breath of air would stir them, the locked hands as though they might move to brush away a fly, and even the artificial eyes, cunningly set under half-dropped eyelids, seemed to regard her from the profound depths of a living peace.

Strange scene! The shadowy cellar. The amber blotch of light. Within its pale effulgence, John Blake, ineffably serene. Upon its borders, the two children, held for an instant within a spell. Cornelia of the glossy pigtails, so slim, so lightly gentle, so intently absorbed; Miad wide-eyed, shock-headed, sturdy, holding firmly her palpitating wrist. He let it go and left her. Unaware that she gazed upon a masterpiece of the embalmer's art, she stood entranced while he fetched a soft cloth from a cranny in the wall and proceeded to dust off his father.

"Miad," she whispered, "who is it?"

"My father," answered Miad with pride. "His name is John Blake."

There was a long pause; then Cornelia murmured with the genuine pathos of orphaned childhood, "How wonderful to have a father, Miad."

Miad nodded gravely and with a quick turn of his head made his bid for atonement. "You can have half of him, Cornelia. He'll be ours together."

"Really, Miad?" cried Cornelia, clutching his hand impulsively. "Really?" As Miad again gravely nodded his head she added solemnly, "And you may call me Corny—when we're alone."

How did she know what Miad was about? Why did she instantly connect self-sacrifice with half-forgotten offense? How do children know anything?

"All right," said Miad with prompt acceptance. "Now you better go home because I've got to work anyway. And you won't tell nothing about coming here. You'll never tell anything ever forever, will you?"

"Never forever," declared Cornelia earnestly. "Forever, Miad."

Meeting her fervent gaze, Miad measured the strength of her avowal and was content. To avoid the rude stable hand he led her through the short cut of Hague Street to Pearl and grinned at her amazement at finding herself so quickly on familiar ground.

"So long, Corny."

"So long, Miad," answered Cornelia happily, waved her hand and ran, her black-stockinged, spindling legs carrying her swiftly on her belated way.

The work to which Miad had referred was real but fantastically varied. He had to keep the rubbish on the premises within bounds— that is, out of Crabbe's and his own way. He had to arrange the rough groundwork and wiring for bird and reptile mountings. He had to prepare the boards for the binding of books in grotesquely rare leathers, tanned by hand. He had to open and unpack the strangest assortment of cases from foreign parts which ever gathered from the corners of the world to enter a single door. Also at the signal of the lifting of one of Crabbe's shaggy eyebrows, it was his office to dodge out unnoticed and run some mysterious chance caller to his final earth.

The atmosphere of combined secrecy and investigation that enveloped Crabbe's establishment was phenomenal, but it was the only air that Miad had breathed from the day of his birth. He was so native to it that old man

Crabbe, once he had drummed into the boy as a baby the cardinal virtues of keeping his mouth shut, trusted him literally without limits. He rarely told him anything, but he let him find all things out. He never said "Don't"; not even at the apparition of Cornelia. Miad had brought her; sequitur and ad hoc, Miad knew what he was about.

It followed that Cobbled Court remained for Miad, day after day and year after year, an inexhaustible source of breathless discoveries, which were unearthed only to be reburied more deeply than ever in the profundities of his own odd being. Instance the day when he spent a hard-earned dime on one of the swarm of Bowery museums which were the illegitimate descendants of Mr. P. T. Barnum's fantastic gold mine over on Broadway, and discovered with deep chagrin that the prize freak was a familiar object, lately elaborated by himself and old man Crabbe. He did not ask for the return of his dime; he did not even recount to Crabbe the amazing revelation. He merely added it to the growing wealth of desultory information that was his stock in trade.

For all his manifold activities Miad received as recompense what in this day and generation would be considered slavery wages. Like his father before him, he was allowed to live rent free in Crabbe's pleasant second-story front. He was further permitted to share in such food as Crabbe himself indulged in. He was regaled from time to time with such oddments of clothing as would save him from going entirely naked in summer and from freezing to death in winter. At equally irregular intervals he was handed a shining silver dollar, which gave him no thrill, as he had early been taught to deposit it in the Bowery Savings Bank. In addition to these emoluments he had the comfort of Mr. Crabbe's frequent and solemn avowal that Miad was his partner; but of his greatest asset he was wholly unconscious. It consisted in the fact that the old man truly regarded him with silent affection and unbounded admiration as his natural heir.

GREAT VAN SUTTART MYSTERY

As the months passed, dotted now and then by Cornelia's snatched visits to exercise her half share in the remains of John Blake, and lengthening swiftly in retrospect into years, Miad grew very rapidly in knowledge but slowly in stature. By the time he was thirteen and Cornelia eleven he was so expert that he could almost have run the shop alone. Almost, but not quite, for there was a sinister aspect to Crabbe's establishment that Miad had often sensed and yet never fully comprehended. Time and again he had felt more than the usual thrill at some startling discovery and known something akin to relief when it did not sweep away at a stroke all mystery. It must not be thought, however, that the word "sinister" would have meant anything to him had he heard it. Nothing so definite as that. He only knew instinctively that a surprise of some kind was long overdue —a surprise that would explain many unsolved quiet comings and goings of mysterious patrons who invariably ignored him.

MIAD SHARES HIS TREASURE

At last it came, though he was not to recognize it at first sight. It arrived on a drowsy Saturday afternoon in the shape of a large case, which was unexpectedly cleared from the customhouse and delivered at Crabbe's shop, where, after much trouble, it was deposited in the cellar near the body of the perpetuated John Blake. Miad was out at the time and it was late on Sunday before he discovered the box during his daily visit for the purpose of dusting off his father. He wondered why Crabbe had said nothing about the arrival, and decided that the old man must have thought the opening of the case too big a job for him to handle. That idea was enough to set him promptly to work. He studied all the stenciled markings with care, made sure that the large box was right side up and, after considerable labor, succeeded in unscrewing its face. After removing all struts and clamps save those in the rear, he took out the packing and found himself face to face with the mounted head of a sable antelope clamped to the back of the box.

GREAT VAN SUTTART MYSTERY

To a layman nothing could have appeared more natural than the mounted head thus held in the exact position it would occupy on a wall; but Miad was not a layman, he was an expert. By the stencilings he had learned that the case came from Africa. Such heads are not usually shipped mounted; they come in three packages, namely—the mask, the skull, the horns. Another thing puzzled him. The mounting was not a rough job, sent to Crabbe for correction; it was the work of a master taxidermist, and to Miad's discriminating eye bore the handicraft hallmark of a famous London house. Yet it had come from Africa.

He decided to remove the head, which could not weigh less than fifty pounds and which, with its splendid curved horns, measured fully four feet in a straight line from brisket to points. First he tipped the packing case back to an angle that would prevent the head's falling forward on its nose and braced the box firmly against a trestle. Then he climbed under and unbolted first the lower two of the four clamps and finally the upper. The head was thus released. Going around to the front he grasped it at the base of the horns and tugged. When he pulled, the case came forward and settled flatly on the floor again. He worked the head out inch by inch, and as soon as the horns were free of the sides of the box he let the heavy trophy down on its back so that the eyes stared up at the ceiling. It now remained only to drag it completely out of the case. As he gave a final tug one of the horns slipped from its core and came off in his hands.

There was nothing surprising about that and he was about to slip it on again when he noticed that the core had been sawed off several inches from the tip. He thought for a minute, took off the other horn and found its core intact. He thought again, picked up a bit of wire, measured it along the length of the truncated core, thrust it into the cavity of the first horn, met an obstacle, twisted the wire until it caught, and then pulled. A wad of paper came out and, tumbling after it, a small

oblong package. Miad picked it up and unwrapped it, disclosing a bottle an inch square,
two inches deep and with a wide neck, tightly
corked. He held it up against the dim light
of the begrimed window. Inside he could
make out three huge black pills, almost as
large as marbles. On the side of the bottle was
a label with a prescription blank filled in with
green ink. He spelled the words out slowly:
"Important: Dissolve in the mouth, one every
hour."

CHAPTER VI

MIAD TAKES HIS FIRST THIRD DEGREE

STRANGE are the sources of suggestion. Even before he had read the unrevealing inscription Miad was seized with an unreasoning desire for possession of the bottle and its contents. Here was mystery indeed. Who had hidden the small package so cunningly? And why? And when? But the suggestion that urged him to keep it for his own did not arise from covetousness, nor had he any sense of wrongdoing. The pills looked like marbles; more than that, they looked like bull's-eyes, the aristocrats of the miggles arena.

Now miggles to Miad at thirteen suggested playing for keeps in contrast to the baby game of finkeeps, and the thought of playing for keeps suggested in turn the cardinal law of boyhood, findings is keepings.

He decided to keep his findings against the world and looked around for a safe hiding place. He thought for a long time, a very long time, for there was nobody on the island of Manhattan at that time who knew better than himself the intricacies of the art of hiding successfully an object however small. Finally a smile quirked the corners of his set lips and a gleam lighted up his eyes. As it happened, he was temporarily reduced to wearing a pair of Mr. Crabbe's discarded corduroy trousers, tightly belted as high as they would go and also rolled up a foot at the bottom to keep them from dragging. He undid one pants leg, placed the bottle within its folds and rolled it up again.

For a moment he loafed complacently, and then was seized by a near-panic at the thought that Mr. Crabbe might surprise him before he could reassemble the sable head. Its dismounting had seemed an impossible job for a boy of his size, but even so he now faced undaunted the herculean task of replacing it. By force of circumstances he was unlike most boys in several ways and in one above all others—efficiency, in the sense of attainment, was part and parcel of his make-up. Crabbe had taught him thoroughness, but the mania for getting things done—that was Miad's own, born in him.

Who had toddled in a straight line? Miad in diapers. Who had walked erect to the thing he wanted and taken it? Miad at three. Who had found a key and purposefully waited until he grew up to the keyhole? Miad—the same Miad who now with unbounded ingenuity and an intuitive knowledge of leverages had just succeeded after an hour's hard labor in reclamping the head and tilting the case to its erect position when Mr. Crabbe came down the stairway from the shop.

"You, Miad?" he asked as he paused to accustom his eyes to the shadowy gloom.

"Sure," said Miad, sagaciously throwing a

few wisps of packing into the box to make it look as if it had not been tipped forward. "Lay a hold of this head while I unclamp it."

The old man approached slowly, so slowly that Miad felt a first tingling thrill.

"Leave that one till tomorrow," said Mr. Crabbe after a long pause during which his shrewd eyes had taken in every detail of evidence as to how far the work of unpacking had progressed. "Come along of me and eat your supper."

Now it was unlike Mr. Crabbe to worry as to whether anyone, himself included, ate or did not eat; consequently Miad lost no time in leaving the ill-provided table and retiring to the refuge of his own room, which was innocent of lamp or candle. He was supposed to undress by feel and to get up whenever day dawned, and on this night he welcomed the dark. After lying in bed for a long cautious hour he reached out for his trousers, unwrapped the bottle and finally succeeded in uncorking it. He rolled one of the pills out into the palm of his hand and popped in into his mouth.

To his surprise the ball was not smooth like an agate to the touch of his tongue; it was stickily rough, as though it had been dipped in paste and then rolled in a powdered licorice. Furthermore its taste was nasty, and he was about to spit it out when a strange feeling of ineffable smoothness was telegraphed by his senses to his brain. What was smoother than the surface of a glass marble? Where had he felt that delectable texture at least once before? Where? Cornelia's wrist? Absurd! His mother's cheek? Impossible! He heard or imagined a creaking on the stairs. Rapidly he replaced the wet pill, drove in the cork, rolled the bottle in the pants leg and threw the trousers from him. No one came, and while he listened he fell asleep, to dream over and over again that someone was in the room, battling for possession of his trousers. In the morning he tried to slip off very early to school, but Mr. Crabbe stopped him.

"Hang around a bit, Miad," he said casually. "I want you should mind the shop."

At half past eight o'clock a butter ball of a man arrived whom Miad recognized as a rare frequenter of the shop. He had trailed him on his own initiative one day and knew that he came from Maiden Lane. He was greasy, soggy and porous like a sponge. Miad had not only hated him on sight but despised him, for, even at the age of eight, he had felt that with the aid of heels and teeth and no interference he could lick him.

Crabbe received the visitor with a non-committal grunt and promptly took him down to the cellar. Miad listened at the head of the stairway. His sharp ears defined every movement of the two men. He felt them pause before the case, heard the stranger exclaim with annoyance and Crabbe explain in return that no one but the kid had touched the box. Then came telltale sounds which indicated that they were freeing the trophy with far more celerity than care. He heard the head thump, and then a rasping sound as it must have pitched forward and slithered on the curve of its horns. What kind of unpacking was that? Presently he heard stirrings amid the strewn packing, and the deliberate, purposeful movements which indicated a systematic search of the entire cellar.

An hour went by. Suddenly the porous stranger gave vent to an angry grunt of exhausted patience and ran for the stairs. Hearing him coming on in spite of a protesting cry from Mr. Crabbe, Miad drew back to the middle of the shop and waited.

The man arrived at the head of the steps, purple in the face and all but breathless. Followed closely by Mr. Crabbe, who was neither flushed nor blown, he advanced menacingly on Miad and with his eyes popping out to match his protuberant stomach, whispered hoarsely, "Come on, now! Out with it! What do you know?"

"What's the use of that, Mr. Levis?" broke in old Crabbe's unemotional voice. "Listen to me, now. Look at him and remember the weight of the head. How could a kid of his size take it out and tack it up again? Tell me that. And if he didn't take it out, he couldn't pull off a horn, now could he?"

Miad's heart was pounding so that for a moment he could not have spoken, even had he wished. It seemed to him that his left leg— the leg with the bottle—was weighted with ball and chain, and that if he should try to run, or even move, the room would be filled with a clanking noise. Without taking his wide eyes off those of the infuriated stranger he reached backward gropingly and laid a hand for support on the workbench on which he had sat hour upon hour as a three-year-old, watching Mr. Crabbe work and listening to Mr. Crabbe discourse on the supreme value of knowing how to keep one's mouth shut.

Echoes were in the room, echoes of Crabbe's voice of long ago: "That mummy there is a tasty trifle, so it is. Spices is in it, natron, gums of Araby, maltha. And honey. Nothing less. But mark me. The honey's been there two thousand years."

Mr. Levis' angry voice broke in upon Miad's recollection. "Why don't he say something if he's so all-fired innocent?" he demanded hotly.

A pause, a fleeting pause, but to Miad filled to the brim with echo; "All them things has been there two thousand years, the mummy has been there two thousand years. Think o' that; and can you tell me why? Because it knows how to keep its mouth shut. Ha! That's it; that's the boy!"

Then Mr. Crabbe, patient, confidently calm, replying in his everyday voice to Mr. Levis, "He will say something, won't you Miad? You didn't take the sable head out of the box, did you now?"

Miad looked to right and left and was on the point of pouring out the truth to his ancient partner when his eyes fell on the Egyptian mummy in the corner. All the drastic training in silence to which it had given point through all the conscious years of his life seemed to surge suddenly within him and, added to the wave, swelling it to vast proportions, came an access of hatred for Mr. Levis which made Miad's face turn red and his lips white. Then silent echo again. Something seemed to burst inside his head into great letters of light: "Keep your mouth shut and your ears open and nothing won't never leak out of us no more than out of that mummy!"

"Two thousand years," he muttered sullenly, and closed his mouth tight.

At the words a look of astonishment swept across Mr. Crabbe's face. His complacent calm left him with a staggering suddenness. He reeled; then came to life and went into action.

"So!" he cried. "So!"

He seized Miad by the arms and with surprising strength lifted and seated him solidly on the workbench. Cunning as a fox was the old man, even in his calmest moments, and now he was aroused. Those three cabalistic words,

MIAD TAKES THIRD DEGREE

"Two thousand years," had waked him as though to the crash and blaze of lightning. Without letting go his hold he leaned forward and felt all Miad's pockets with his elbows, talking quietly as he did so.

"Now, Miad, this ain't one of the times. Do you understand me? You can open your mouth, Miad. You can say all you know, right here in front of Mr. Levis. Spill it. Who was in here? Who helped you with the sable head? I tell you this ain't one of the times, Miad. You can speak. I want you should speak."

At each sentence Mr. Crabbe gave his diminutive partner a shake of increasing violence, but a quaver began to creep into the old man's voice in proportion as he gathered the significance of the viselike set of Miad's lips and realized that to pry them open he would first have to undo the training of many years.

Appreciating almost at once the futility of argument, he fell back on dogged perseverance and, tightening his hold, repeated over and over again, "I want you should speak."

After half an hour, during which the staring, granitelike expression on Miad's face had never once flickered into life, Mr. Levis exclaimed, "Aw, let me get at him!"

"Stay off," commanded Crabbe as he felt a sudden quiver run through Miad's compact little body.

Had anyone chanced to enter the shop on that Monday morning during the two hours which ensued he would have stood rooted to the floor at the spectacle of a very small boy on the workbench, shockheaded, glassy-eyed, white of face and whiter of lips, imprisoned by the grip of the weary and sweating white-haired Mr. Crabbe and fusilladed by hoarse shouts and angry ejaculations from a porous, goggle-eyed and paunchy individual who hopped around first on one foot and then on the other, and occasionally shot out a pudgy hand to feel the boy's pockets or peck at his tattered clothing.

MIAD TAKES THIRD DEGREE

"Let me at him, the dirty little swipe! Choke him! Wring his cursed little neck. Crabbe, if you don't squeeze it out of him I'll blacken your name from here to Turkestan. Yah! Honest Crabbe! Bond-word Crabbe! You think I can't have the law on the two of you. Not for this, perhaps; but just the same, I'll run you out of house and home. By all the beards of the prophets, I'll—"

Utterly exhausted, old man Crabbe released his hold to draw out a vast bandanna and mop his dripping brow. Instantly Mr. Levis saw his chance and pounced on Miad. Never in his cunning, weasel-like existence had he made a more grievous error. At the clutch of his stumpy hands the immobile boy became a blazing ball of fury. He kicked, he bit, he scratched. He drove the sharp corners of his heels scrapingly down Mr. Levis' shins, and his teeth into the fat of Mr. Levis' thumb. Far from attempting to escape, he clung to Mr. Levis with all the varied tentacles of his incredibly powerful little body, meanwhile tearing at clothing and flesh with a rage that was elemental and terrifying, all the more so since it came from so small a source.

"Take him off!" howled Mr. Levis piteously as soon as he could catch a breath.

Mr. Crabbe seemed paralyzed by the turn of events. He stood with his steel-rimmed glasses pushed high up into his disheveled hair and washed his thin hands one within the other with a tight, nervous movement; but in his deep-set eyes under the twitching shaggy brows there was a gleam—or was it a twinkle? —which neither of the combatants had leisure or opportunity to observe. It was as though Mr. Crabbe, his patience exhausted in two diametrically opposed directions and his duty at war with his inclination, were enjoying himself heartily by proxy.

"Oh, Miad," cried the old man chokingly from time to time, "please stop! Please don't Miad! Miad, you mustn't; you really mustn't."

Without warning, Miad suddenly released

his many holds, drew back, lowered his head and drove it with the force of a battering-ram into Mr. Levis' paunch; then he turned and ran for the door. Now Mr. Levis had just one quality in his make-up which transcended bodily fear, and its name was pertinacity. At the foul blow he doubled up like a jackknife, but when, upon straightening, his eyes caught the flicker of Miad's disappearing form he promptly set out in pursuit. He reached the door within a few seconds of starting and with a single glance took in the complete emptiness of Cobbled Court. Equally swift deduction told him that only the gaping door of Maclintock's stables could have swallowed the fugitive so quickly.

At that very instant Miad was standing pantingly on one foot, just within the dark passage from stable to warehouse, and feeling feverishly for the treasure rolled in his left trouser leg. It was safe; far from being lost or discovered, the bottle had not even been broken in the furious mêlée, so snugly had his astuteness packed it away. But his relief was not quite complete. As he had bolted into the stable he had been forced to dive between the legs of Mike, the mucker-out of unpleasant memory, upsetting him with a thud. Consequently Miad waited expectantly for the word of betrayal. Presently came Mr. Levis' weakly explosive voice:

"Where's the kid that run in here?"

"There ain't no kid run in here, mister," drawled the stable hand in reply. "Not as I know of. Nobody ain't allowed in the stables without Mr. Maclintock says so. If you mean that scalawag of a Miad Blake—why, I seen him scuttlin' down Cliff Street not a minute ago, and I sure hope you catch him an' lick the tar out of him for what he done to your nice clothes."

"Cliff Street, nothin'," muttered Mr. Levis.

Feeling a warm thrill of gratitude which changed completely his former estimate of the stable hand, Miad crept through the corridor, threaded his way among the bales of hides into Vandewater Street, and then ran as fast as his legs could carry him. By the position of various children whom he met on their way home to lunch, he knew exactly how long school was out. He scampered up the New Bowery to East Broadway and breathlessly hailed Cornelia just as she was seizing the bell pull of the pompous but gloomy home in which she lived. After one glance at Miad's troubled perspiring face she ran down the steps and around the corner into the comparative privacy of Market Street.

"Oh, Miad! What is it?" she asked as he joined her.

He stooped over, retrieved the little bottle and, without looking at it, pressed it into her hand. "Hide it, Corny," he gulped. "Forever. You know."

The next moment he was gone as fast as he had come. He passed Vandewater, Hague Street and Brooklyn Bridge. Within twenty minutes of his escape he sauntered nonchalantly up Cliff Street, into the great arch and through the ramshackle gate of Cobbled Court, directly in the vision of the astonished Mr. Levis, who was sitting with dogged patience on a box beside the entrance to the Maclintock stables.

"Where you been?" demanded Mr. Levis vapidly, too confounded to rise.

"None of your business," replied Miad calmly as he dodged into the shop.

During the weeks that followed, the whole atmosphere of Cobbled Court became electrically charged. Certain of its habitués went around in a cautious daze, as though to poke out a finger carelessly would be to get a shock; and the dead center of the static disturbance was no less a person than Miad Blake, aged thirteen, who was watched night and day, not only by Mr. Levis and certain of Mr. Levis' shady agents, but far more intelligently by the canny Mr. Crabbe. In fact, the old man did more than watch. He talked at length when the two were alone on the theme of the honor of the house of Crabbe, how its word had ever been its bond, and on the fact that even the iron rule of knowing how to keep one's mouth shut had its exceptions. At such times Miad would fasten his eyes on a certain corner of the shop and hold them there so fixedly that Mr. Crabbe was more than once driven to the ejaculation, "Gol dast that gol-durned mummy!"

It was part and parcel of Miad's precocious perspicacity that during these same weeks he had spoken to Cornelia only once, and that on an occasion when he was sure they were unobserved.

"Say Corny," he asked with suppressed excitement, "did you look at what's in the bottle?"

"Of course," replied Cornelia. "From the outside."

"Well," demanded Miad, "what is they?"

"Two balls, very dark brown, almost black; and one white one, Miad. Whiter than white, like a swan in the park with a light inside.

You think it's pinky, almost; but it isn't, really. Just white. Lovely."

Miad was awed; he did not know why, but he was awed. Not by her words in themselves, but because they capped a momentous string of sensations, beginning with the size of Mr. Levis' initial rage and continuing with the sense that he, Miad Blake, was tampering with huge things—things like jaws that once clamped would never let go. His teeth set tight and he let a whole month pass before he spoke to Cornelia again, and then it was only to say, "You better come around first chance you get. The old man said it was kind of queer he hadn't seen you so long. But you remember, Corny, forever and forever."

CHAPTER VII

"POLICE!" SCREAMED CORNY

ALL women are born pinch hitters at the art
of acting, and Cornelia was no exception.
When she entered Crabbe's shop on the ensu-
ing Saturday afternoon she carried within her
small breast a great burden of guilt, of curiosity and of the tremors of a conspirator, but
her exterior betrayed none of these things.
She was as light and gravely gay as she had
been on each of the rare occasions when opportunity had enabled her to accompany Miad to
Cobbled Court. This time she had come alone.

"Mr. Crabbe," she asked at the very moment
of greeting, "is Miad mad at me?"

Mr. Crabbe stared at her long and thoughtfully over his glasses. For days he had been

mulling certain queries which he meant to pro-
pound to this slip of a girl at their first encounter, and now her single question made him
feel like a spiked gun!

"No," he grunted; "not as I know on.
Why?"

"Well," said Cornelia, letting fall her curling lashes, "I hardly ever see him any more,
and he doesn't ask me to come here like he
used to. You don't mind me being here, do you,
Mr. Crabbe?"

Mr. Crabbe started to say that little girls
were a drug on the market as far as he per-
sonally was concerned, but suddenly reflected
that he had been wishing for some time for a
leisurely sight of this particular little girl, so
he changed a drawling "Well—" into "Why,
no. Just you play around until Miad comes
along. You say you ain't seen him lately?"

Apparently Cornelia had not heard the
question. She paid no attention to it. Its sole
effect was to make her pause at the nearest
thing instead of going on to her favorite, the

stuffed dugong, and the nearest thing happened to be the table laden with exotic journals. She began to turn them over absentmindedly. Mr. Crabbe watched her, perceived that she was genuinely killing time, and turned to resume his work. Had he watched one-fifth of a second longer he would have seen her body slowly tauten into a petrified stillness. Presently Miad entered.

"Hello, Cornelia."

"Hello, Miad."

"I guess your folks don't know where you are," continued Miad coldly.

"And I bet you don't know how to spell hippopotamus," said Cornelia with a challenging nervous laugh.

"Huh! Don't I though?" said Miad, and spelled the word promptly and correctly.

But Cornelia shook her head violently. "That isn't the way it's spelled here," she said.

"Let's see," said Miad, advancing upon her. As he came between Crabbe and herself he saw her press her two index fingers on the pages before her so firmly that the knuckles turned white and the nails bright red.

"There," she cried. "Look for yourself."

Miad leaned over her shoulder. On the left page was a picture of a hippopotamus with the name spelled wrongly through a palpable misprint. On the right page, at the tip of Cornelia's finger, was a small advertisement headed by the word "reward" in bold-faced type and followed by six lines of fine print: "REWARD. £2000 for information leading to the recovery of three matched Oriental pearls of 42½ grains each, shipped to unknown destination together with sable antelope head. No questions asked. £2000!" At the end came an unpronounceable and almost unreadable address in Amsterdam.

"What you got there?" demanded Mr. Crabbe, sensing a sudden tense stillness.

Miad picked up the journal. Feeling as if he carried his life in his hands he approached the old man. He pointed at the misspelled word with a finger which he kept from trem-

bling only by a superhuman effort and demanded, "Is that right, Crabbe, or ain't
it?"

"It ain't," declared Mr. Crabbe, peering
painfully at the indistinct print. "Now, you
get out of here, both on you. Bothering me
with spelling lessons."

Miad dropped the journal, kicked it through
the door and ran after it with a whoop. Cornelia followed. They pounced on the paper.
They tugged at and tore it, but with method.
Leaving the balance of the crumpled volume
on the ground, Miad crammed a rolled ball of
a page or two into his pocket. As soon as they
were in Hague Street and he had assured himself that they were out of hearing of all and
sundry, he demanded, "How did you know,
Corny? You tell me how you knew them was
it."

Cornelia shook her head. "I don't know how
I knew. I just knew; that's all."

"No, you didn't," persisted Miad. "You
couldn't. How could you? I never told you

nothing about the sable head. Now you tell me. How did you know?"

"Oh, Miad," said Cornelia, throwing up her head, "please don't be cross! It said on the bottle, 'Important: Dissolve in the mouth'; so I did, only because it said important in big letters, Miad. And they were all whiter than white, and lovely. All of them. Three of them. And so—I knew. I just knew; that's all. Are you cross, Miad?"

"Gee, no," answered Miad. "I guess something will happen pretty soon, Corny. You run along home, because I got something to do."

He returned to Cobbled Court, joked with the teamsters in Maclintock's stable for a minute, entered the stable, issued on Vandewater Street and ran for the post office. There he bought two stamped envelopes, wastefully using one for his letter. "A schoolboy named Miad Blake at Public School No. 112 in Roosevelt Street knows about pearls and sable head," he wrote, stuffed the note into the second envelope, took out the torn sheets from his pocket, found the advertisement and laboriously printed the Amsterdam address. He then sealed and mailed the letter, blissfully ignorant of the fact that its recipient would have to pay double postage.

During four weeks Miad and Cornelia grew daily thinner and paler with suspense and worry, but for Miad the period of stress was broken by an epochal event. As he passed through Hague Street one day the narrow door of one of the houses opened to emit a hurrying figure and almost instantly closed again; but in the flash of the interval Miad had seen the following things: Three steep steps, a high floor, a bare table in a small bare room and, standing like a dim white wraith, Mr. Crabbe, counting a wad of money.

Miad hurried home, trying to pretend even to himself that he had not seen, but muttering under his breath, "So that's it—that's the house—that's where it comes out." Memories of the underground passage assailed him and the usual lump came into his throat as he thought of his mother, remembering the breathing smoothness of her cheek like the living surface of a pearl, once felt upon his tongue, never forgotten. Pearls and women, mysterious, warm, deep—things far apart, and yet akin! The very next day as he came out of school at the noon hour, a boy called, "Hi! Miad! Here's a gent wants to see you."

Miad paused in midstep, turned, dashed back into the hall and drew Cornelia aside. "Corny," he whispered excitedly, "you meet me in Market Street in fifteen minutes and bring it. You know."

Then he ran out to accost the stranger. He found a very calm individual, exceedingly well dressed, with olive-tinted cheeks and two jet-black eyes that twinkled with mirth and shrewdness.

"You come from Amsterdam?" murmured Miad out of the corner of his mouth and staring at nothing in particular.

"Well, not recently," replied the stranger

with an amused smile. "But I have had a letter from Amsterdam authorizing me to deal with a schoolboy named Miad Blake."

"Me's him," declared Miad unsmilingly, "and I've got you-know-what, only I won't give it to you in the street where you can cut and run. You got the nerve to go somewhere I say after school?"

The stranger's smile broadened. "Yes," he answered presently, "I have the nerve."

"Listen," said Miad. "Somebody's watching of us this minute, see? You walk through Hague Street at ten minutes after three. Go south from here on Pearl. Hague Street is the first after Vandewater to the right. Got it?"

"Yes," said the stranger, his face sobering. "You certainly have a clear head and a clearer tongue, youngster."

"Never mind me being a youngster," said Miad belligerently. "You come alone and bring the money or you won't get nothin' but a look."

At exactly ten minutes past three the

stranger turned from Pearl into Hague Street, unconscious that he was being shadowed by a girl of eleven with hidden, excited eyes and two glossy pigtails. Suddenly his unruffled calm suffered a severe jolt. A great key rasped in the lock of a narrow door, the door swung outward, almost knocking him off his feet, and Miad's voice said, "Hop up, and be quick about it."

The man barely hesitated before he ran up the three steep steps and stood wondering just what kind of a fool he was making of himself while Miad locked the door, pocketed the huge key and lit the stub of a candle. By its light the boy looked so very small that the stranger felt reassured enough to follow him down a steep stairway and around a turn into a vaulted chamber which, God be praised, was dimly lighted by an iron grating at the level of the street. In the center of the underground chamber was a scarred workbench. Miad advanced, set the candle on it, crooked one knee, unrolled his trouser leg, took out the bottle and

held it for a revealing instant before the flame.
Within the bottle glowed softly three luminous
spheres of imprisoned light. The stranger's
eyes flamed, and then melted almost to a look
of adoration, but he did not move.

"I guess perhaps they're worth more than
two thousand pounds," breathed Miad, his
own gaze held by the most subtle of all fascina-
tions.

"More; much more," murmured the
stranger. "Ten times more; but only to the
one person who can sell them honestly."

On the last word his voice suddenly hard-
ened, his head went up with a jerk, and his jet-
black eyes seemed to shoot forked lightning
into the far shadows of the room. His lips
drew back to snarl with the rage of betrayal.
Miad looked up at the man's contorted face
and immediately felt as though an icicle had
touched his spine. His fingers closed spasmodically over the bottle. His eyes swerved
slowly, inexorably, toward the mouth of the
cavernous passage which led toward Cobbled

Court. Two shadowy figures were emerging from it stealthily, stealing one to the right, one to the left. Creeping—creeping forward. Old man Crabbe, bent like a quivering claw; Mr. Levis, round, moist, venomous as a toad.

Miad's bones seemed to turn to water; all his strength flowed from him, leaving him stranded, pitifully revealed even to himself as a small boy, a very small boy, who had childishly evoked the forces that were about to overwhelm him. Things like jaws were closing upon him— things that once clamped would never let go! Strange events had occurred within these clammy walls. He had always felt it; he knew it now. Old man Crabbe, Mr. Levis—had he ever known them, seen them before? Not like this. They were different, horribly different, silent and purposeful as the gleam of a flashing knife. He cast an anxious glance at the stairway, but already it was too late to flee, and, besides, there was the locked door—locked on him and on the stranger.

Something was about to happen—something

horrible. Never in his life had he formed a conception of murder, but he formed it now, instantly, full-fledged. It hung in the air, heavy, wet, like an oozing blanket, making him gasp to get his breath. They were not looking at him—Crabbe and Mr. Levis. No. Their eyes were pinned like needles on the stranger. He—Miad—that would come after.

Tears of bitter disillusionment started rolling down his cheeks. He was so small—so very small! Then from the depths of his being, quite suddenly, his combative soul came into its own again. Rage filled him, such a rage as he had never before known. What did they take him for? Hadn't he thought things out? He would show them, these men! Let the trap he had laid for the stranger engulf them all. By a mighty effort he swallowed the tears that were choking him, and coughed. It was a weak, gurgling cough, but it was enough.

Instantly there sounded through the quivering silence a clear, treble voice: "Miad, shall I call the police?"

GREAT VAN SUTTART MYSTERY

There was something blood freezing in the words as they shattered the stillness above the tense group. Astoundingly sudden. Incredibly near. A voice—all by itself, coming from no one, from nowhere; incorporeal, eerie, detached! Crabbe, claw extended, ceased to move. Mr. Levis no longer oozed; he coagulated, looking green, slimy to the touch. The stranger jerked and turned to stone. Miad alone lived. His heart pounded and swelled almost to bursting as he threw back his head and called clearly "Yes!"

"Police!" screamed Cornelia with all the strength of her lungs.

The loud cry caromed from one stone wall of the tomb-like chamber to another till mighty echo swallowed echo. With a hoarse cry of terror Mr. Levis turned and fled, scurrying and slithering through the cavernous passage like a fat rat. Followed him Mr. Crabbe, calling acidly as he went, "Don't run, you fool! There ain't a cop within a mile of here!"

Miad heard an explosive chuckle and looked

around in amazement. The stranger had not run. He was holding his sides and laughing as only the brave know how to laugh.

As soon as he could speak he stammered, "For heaven's sake, bring your friend in or send her home. I won't cheat you, boy. I don't know how you got the Luxendorf pearls and I don't care. Here's nine thousand seven hundred and thirty-three dollars. Count it and hand over the bottle."

As he spoke he tossed a large package of bank notes on the bench. Miad clutched the money and with his eyes fastened steadily on those of the stranger called out, "It's all right, Cornelia. Is anybody coming?"

"No one, Miad. There's no one in Hague Street. Shall I run to the corner?" Her quick words reverberated strangely, gobbling each other up.

"No," ordered Miad. "I tell you, it's all right. You run along home, Cornelia. I got the money and I guess I can keep it."

He examined the bills, but did not attempt

to count them. "I guess you're all right, mister. Here's the bottle."

The stranger uncorked it and rolled the three magnificent pearls into the palm of his hand.

"Gee, mister!" gasped Miad. "Leave me look. I ain't never seen 'em."

As he drank in the beauty of the trans-figured black pills, so white, so alive, the memory of his mother came rolling over him in a flood. Here—here in the cellar—just over there, her voice, "Oh baby, my dear, dear boy, why did you run from your mother?" Just over there! He glanced to the left. The spot where he had last seen her, the chamber of their swift farewell, was gone—closed—sealed with a wall of tumbled stones, mortar and earth! "Run, darling! Run!" Then came the stranger's voice, snatching him back from that far-away day.

"Never seen them!" he exclaimed. "What do you mean?"

"Well," explained Miad, "they were covered with black. It tasted like licorice, but I only sucked one and that was in the dark. Cornelia sucked the others."

"Thank God!" murmured the man fervently. "You see, boy, pearls can't live long without air. You and Cornelia may have saved the lives of these beauties, and that isn't all. I don't suppose it will mean much to you now; but when you get older you remember what I'm telling you. You've saved the honor of a royal house. These pearls were stolen by a young man who will be a ruling prince some day, worse luck. What for? I'll tell you that too. To salt a pearl fishery on the coast of Africa. Just a skin game like you or I might try to play if we didn't know better. Now you come with me and put that money where nobody can take it from you."

At the Bowery Savings Bank the stranger's calling card gained them prompt admittance to the manager's office and Miad was introduced with a formality that made him squirm. The manager ruffled the heap of bank notes thoughtfully and pretended that he was not being eaten alive with curiosity.

"How do you wish this money credited, Mr. Blake?" he asked respectfully.

"Aw! Cheese it," retorted Miad. "Who do you think you're kidding? I'm Miad, and you know it."

"Well, Miad," said the manager, smiling, "time deposit with interest or current account and no interest?"

"Time," answered Miad; "and please put one-third to old man Crabbe, one-third to me and one-third to Cornelia Van Suttart."

"Cornelia Van Suttart!" exclaimed the manager, startled out of his assumed calm, his eyes suddenly narrowing. "What do you know about Cornelia Van Suttart?"

"Never you mind what I know about her," replied Miad belligerently. "You just do what I said; and what's more, you can give her the extra cent."

CHAPTER VIII

On a certain warm afternoon in the month
of May of the year 1883, had a passerby
chanced to enter the single block of Hague
Street in the city of New York at fourteen
minutes after four, he would have seen the
following things: An ancient two-seated surrey with the top removed. A fat somnolent
dray horse between the shafts of the said surrey. A narrow door that opened outward until
it struck the front wheel of the surrey. Three
steep steps. A man, who smelled strongly of
the stables, tugging at a box of strange yet
familiar shape, loosely covered with a checkered tablecloth. Lastly and most important of
all, his wondering gaze would have beheld a
small, perspiring profoundly reverent boy

named Miad Blake, pushing with all his strength at the other end of the casket.

But wait a minute or an hour or two. People do not transfer a loaded casket into the back seat of a ramshackle surrey without due cause, and Miad had been accumulating justification for removing the perpetuated remains of his father, John Blake, during a period of many feverish weeks. It all began even before the following elucidating discourse on the part of old man Crabbe, who, at the time of speaking, may be pictured as standing in a characteristic pose in his strange shop in Cobbled Court.

Steel-rimmed specs in peril at the very end of his nose. Disheveled white hair. Chin dropped on his thin chest. Beside him the scarred workbench upon which Miad as a baby had been born into consciousness of strange things as they are. Behind him the said strange things: The stuffed dugong; the cases upon cases of beasts of the forest, reptiles of the sea and birds of the air; the trachomatous goldfish and the sphinxlike Egyptian mummy which had lasted for two thousand years because it knew how to keep its mouth shut.

Incidentally, the mummy, especially its infinite capacity for stubborn silence, was in disgrace. "Mark my words," said Mr. Crabbe, his gray gimlet eyes boring into Miad, who was standing on his left leg like a stork and rubbing its calf nervously with the instep of his right foot—"mark my words, I say. You done a lot to me and a lot to the shop and a lot to your own self when you picked on that fat pig-eyed Mr. Levis to steal his pearls."

"They weren't his pearls, and I didn't steal 'em," burst out Miad, his eyes flashing battle as he quickly planted both feet solidly on the floor.

"Easy! Easy, now," remarked Mr. Crabbe placidly as he elevated his chin, focused his eyes through the distant lozenges of his glasses and straightened a pinfeather of the rare bird he was mounting with the tweezers held in his expert right hand. He continued to talk as he worked. "No. You're right. You didn't steal nothing. I'll say that for you to my dying hour. And them pearls didn't belong to Mr. Levis except in a manner of speaking. Free and easy, you might say they did belong to him most particular until you come snooping around, meddling with none of your business and blowing up as nice a little arrangement as two hard-working, earnest men ever laid against the wants of old age and a rainy day."

"Free and easy!" scoffed Miad, unmoved by Mr. Crabbe's ludicrously plaintive tone. "You and your Mr. Levis!" His belligerent eyes visualized so distinctly the detested Mr. Levis that he spat at him. "You ought to be ashamed on yourself."

"Yes," agreed Mr. Crabbe abstractedly, "I reckon I had ought, and many is the time. But not for a quiet little matter of business like them pearls. No, sir. Other things."

He nodded, paused in his work, and for an instant his deep-set eyes gleamed so balefully that Miad felt a cold shiver trickle up his spine and down again.

"What things?" he asked.

The old man shot a look at him and then came to himself. "Did I ever tell you anything?" he asked sharply. "Teach you, yes. I've learned you all I knowed, from how to keep your mouth shut to the true set of a frigate bird's wing, but I ain't never told you nothing, now have I? You found out things for your own good and some for your own bad, but the first time you finds out something that smells big and ugly to you, what do you do? You show an honest streak and annoy Mr. Levis."

"You called him pig-eyed," remarked Miad, as though the statement explained his entire position.

"So I did and so he is," admitted Mr. Crabbe, and continued: "Now, Miad, don't think I'm grousing of you. Honesty is like red hair and the things that goes with red hair. You're born with it or you ain't. If you ain't, you got to learn to take honesty like snuff.

Some on us can do without it all our lives and never miss it. Some on us that naturally does without it grows thin like me, and some fat like Pig Eyes, but I'm old enough to of seen one thing: Them on us as grows fat is always oily. There is some honest fat men and you can tell them by their dry skins, but if you was to drive an old buggy close to Mr. Levis the wheels would stop squeaking."

"You ought to be glad I sneaked them pearls from under him," muttered Miad unsmilingly.

"Glad!" ejaculated Mr. Crabbe. "Ha! You think you was smart. You think that after having his back teeth yanked out, old Pig Eyes is going to sit down and twiddle his thumbs and say, 'Tut, tut! It was only the prank of a blue-eyed kid.' Bah!"

The old man in his turn spat on the floor. Again he shot a piercing glance against the wall of Miad's indifference. "You better wake up. You started something nasty, Miad; and when it's cooked, you and me has got to eat it. You found a keg of powder under the shop and set a honest match to it and blew you and me and our business so high that nothing won't ever come down except cordwood and a bucksaw. From now on and until Mr. Levis dies, you and me has got to work and sweat for a living, so we have."

"Crabbe, what do you mean?" asked Miad, his attention seized. "Is this place illegal?"

"Illegal!" gasped Mr. Crabbe. "Why, son, things has been done here that the law never thought on. Things without no words to 'em, that crawled out of the minds of queer folks as quiet as a white worm. That's it, Miad. White worms with no sound to 'em and only one eye. Why, Sunday-school exercises like stealing slaves from their rightful owners and pearls from Mr. Levis ain't even listed. No, sir. Things that if they was put down in purple ink would take the curl out of all the hair in Africa."

"Murders, Crabbe?" breathed Miad, wide-eyed at last.

"Murders, now," said Mr. Crabbe, pinching his lower lip while his eyes grew vague in recollection. "Awk'ard things, murders. Bad headwork, like you almost made us do the other day. No; not many of them, son. A few here, and more that was brought here—afterwards. You know. But not many. Not over eighteen or twenty."

For a moment Miad thought Crabbe was joking, and started to smile, but his lips twitched and straightened as his eyes were drawn and held by the peculiar opaqueness of the old man's reminiscent gaze. Something began to roll and swell and threaten to slop over inside of Miad. He was not frightened exactly, but he wanted to run away and cry. However, he could not run from anything so familiar and everyday as the white-haired person of Mr. Crabbe. It would be absurd. And as for crying, he had never yet been known to cry except from rage. He surrendered, in the end, to an impulse of propitiation.

"Perhaps you don't know," he gulped, "that

THE FACE AT THE WINDOW

I give the bank one-third of the reward in your name."

"Know it? Of course I know it," said the old man testily. "Didn't I hand over every cent of my share to Mr. Levis to square our name?"

"To Mr. Levis!" cried Miad, his eyes blazing and his cheeks reddening. "You give it to Mr. Levis?"

"Say," said Mr. Crabbe, staring at him in wonder and admiration, "have you got the cheek to get angry at me because you done me out of a business it has took more years than you can count to establish? Miad, where you been while I been talking? Can't you hear when I tell you Pig Eyes has been and sicked the police onto us? Take off your coat."

"I can't," said Miad, subdued. "I got to go to school."

"Oh, no, you ain't," rejoined the old man. "Wake up, Miad. You got to work. You ain't never again going to see the inside of any school; only this here one."

"Not going to school?" gasped Miad. "But I got to. The truant officer will come after me."

"Truant officer!" scoffed Mr. Crabbe. "If a truant officer tried to catch up with you he'd swallow himself and come out through his own feet."

Instantly Miad's bold eyes showed a gleam within their gleam, and as his thoughts ranged rapidly through the maze and the burrow that were Cobbled Court his set lips quirked into a perky smile. Could he dodge any man or any combination of men for an entire year? He could and he would.

"I guess that's right, Crabbe," he murmured complacently. "What you want I should do?"

"The first thing you got to do," said Mr. Crabbe, "is to hang around in the alley and the holes you know so much about, and stop all the queer folks before they get here. Give 'em the high sign. Steer 'em clear and away of the shop. Tell 'em I'm dead."

"How will I know the ones?" asked Miad.

THE FACE AT THE WINDOW

"Know 'em!" exclaimed Crabbe, giving his small parner a mocking glance. "You stringing me, Miad? You'll know 'em by the white worm behind their eyes."

Miad nodded. Already he had solved the problem in his own head.

For days he played around the door of Maclintock's stables or in the gloom of the cavernous alley that flanked Brooklyn Bridge, and for equal days runners from Maiden Lane, absent-minded herpetologists, medical students carrying strange parcels, illicit pharmacopolists, vulpine purveyors of freaks, fraudulent cripples—in short, the whole astounding gamut of the variations in human nature, from the pervert to the erudite and from the gruesome to the guileless, which had made up the vertebræ of the backbone of Mr. Crabbe's business—jumped each in his turn half out of his skin at catching on the wing a whisper from a flying boy.

"Cheese it, mister! The police is in the shop."

GREAT VAN SUTTART MYSTERY

Those who were on honest business bent, recovered their composure and pursued their interrupted way; those of the white worm behind the eyes attained to varying degrees of speed, and vanished down Hague Street, through the arch into Cliff, around the corner into Frankfort, or doubled on Miad's tracks and frankly bolted into the shadows of the cavernous alley to debouch into Vandewater or Hope Street, each of which gave them the option of an escape to the north or the south.

It was a juicy morsel of a game for Miad, luscious on the tongue, and he missed none of its flavor. Within a week, had he been inclined to blackmail, he could have made up a list that would have provided him with a generous annuity, for every crook will pay tribute within reason for freedom from surveillance. The idea, however, never entered his head, even though old man Crabbe missed no chance to bemoan the straitened circumstances that the watchful enmity of Mr. Levis had brought about.

THE FACE AT THE WINDOW

In addition to the need for Mr. Crabbe's working like a beaver on honest trifles, there was the necessity of deflecting certain shipments already on the way from foreign parts, as well as of stopping all compromising patrons short of the premises. As a result, Miad's time was rather pleasantly spent in the open while the old man was chained to his workbench so inexorably that it is amazing to record no noticeable increase in his habitual irascibility. If anything, he seemed to take a sort of inverted joy in the complexities of so ordering his highly susceptible affairs that Mr. Levis might never find a chance to spring the dreaded blue-coated jaws of the law.

This chronicle is written in vain if it has not set forth the fact that Mr. Crabbe was an individual in a period when circumstances made individuals by the ton and then left them around unnoticed like so much scrap iron. Such men are not born of another's fancy. When it is stated that Mr. Crabbe was as lean and dry as a strip of rawhide, that his white hair was habitually rumpled on a high brow by the steel-rimmed glasses that constantly traversed the segment of an arc from the top of his head to the tip of his nose, and that his gimlet eyes were piercing, baleful or humorous as though governed by a switch, no credit whatever is taken for the resulting picture any more than if one should take credit for depicting a Belgian block as something oblong, made of granite and excruciatingly painful to kick with a bare toe.

Far deeper perception is necessary, however, to penetrate the true inwardness of the old man's extraordinary attitude toward Miad. Here we come to grips with the articulations, the intricacies, the very skeleton and sinews of an individual philosophy in action. Set aside, if you can, the confounding attribute of human affection. Forget the toddling baby Miad as three-year-old waif, son of the city of New York, taking everything he wanted by assault, even to a seat, in and out of season, on the workbench in Crabbe's lugubrious shop. Banish these things from mind, fix your eyes on an extremely compact shock-headed Miad of thirteen winters, and perceive the two feet of Crabbe's philosophy set solidly on the rocks of tolerance and respect for the independence of the single soul. Set aside, I say, the confounding attribute of human affection—if you can.

Be that as it may, in all his bemoanings the old man never for a moment quarreled with the motive that had led Miad to filch certain priceless pearls from too close proximity to the snout of Mr. Levis and restore them in exchange for a fair but insignificant reward to their rightful owner. Far from it. The motive, *per se,* filled him with an inordinate pride. All he kicked about was the sudden necessity for arduous and continual labor in barter for small pay. As a result of Mr. Crabbe's acrid remarks on this subject, redolent with the tradition of the curse on the Garden of Eden, Miad pitched whole-heartedly into work as soon as word had filtered through to the outposts of the shop's tainted patronage that

Crabbe was under threat of the law through the pertinacious animosity of a certain Mr. Levis.

Mr. Crabbe's prediction as to the fate of any truant officer who might try to catch Miad failed of fulfillment only because the various monitors of school attendance assigned to the duty preferred to give up the quest rather than swallow themselves and exude through their own feet. The system employed was very simple. Miad was given a workbench in the light of the cellar window that overlooked the perpetuated remains of his father, John Blake. Whenever an officer appeared in the shop above, Mr. Crabbe would look around nervously and drop whatever tool he happened to be working with. At the signal Miad would withdraw into the masked tunnel which had an exit into Hague Street and await developments.

Two diversions served to alleviate the tedium of his life at this time, once the truant officers slackened in their sterile efforts to seize his person: The first was the frequent snooping visits of the porcine Mr. Levis; the other the rare presence of his little playmate and ally, Cornelia Van Suttart. Toward the former Miad was wont to employ a regrettable gesture composed of a thumb and four fingers applied to the nose. Toward Cornelia he evinced a preliminary glow of welcome, followed closely by truculent orders to help him with this and that. To see her obey, abet and aid him was to perceive the working sources of adoring abnegation.

Miad did not love Cornelia, nor did Cornelia love Miad, in any sloppy sense of the word. What they loved, without question and without knowing why, was to be together. There was something breath-taking in the short-skirted swirl of her arrivals. Crabbe's shop, its cellar and, above all, Miad himself seemed charged with a subtle magnetism for her. Whence she came they did not know, beyond the fact that it was out of a sombre house on East Broadway, but they did know that she came with a rush of small wings, as of a bird alighting, and went away with lagging step and backward glance.

So expressive were all her ways that, without a single spoken word on the subject, Miad grew into a consciousness of the damp emptiness of Cornelia's stately home, of the hollowness to her of school since he was gone, and of her quiet radiating joy in being by his side surrounded by the grim mysteries of Cobbled Court. It was good to have her there, to order her about, to pause in his work, stare spellbound into the shadows and whisper hoarsely, "Murders, Corny. Not many. Eighteen or twenty."

Her head would quirk like the head of a bird listening. Her hidden eyes would open wide, deep, profoundly lucent. The pallor of her cheeks would flush with the faint tint of a living petal; and then Miad, taking mean advantage of her abstraction, would steal his hand around behind her back, seize one of her glossy braids and pull it. Shuddering quiver of her body. Caught, gasping breath, and then a gulp, a low cry:

"Miad! Oh! Oh! Miad!"

"Gee! Corny, how you jumped!"

It should not be overlooked that John Blake, preserved, was present in person at all the rare meetings between Miad and Cornelia. The words "in person" mean just that; they are not used figuratively. Something of the essence of the erstwhile porter had not flown with death. It had remained, bound to the things of this earth by the outright love of the boy he had left behind. He was not only present, he was real—a complacent, serene and beloved companion.

On the occasion of Cornelia's visits, the daily dusting off of the waxlike mummy became a ceremony in which she was now allowed to share. The labor of love accomplished, the two children would stand side by side and gaze upon the peaceful, lifelike face with such an expression of simple affection in their faces as only the very young of heart can bestow upon their dearest treasure. On such a trance of child-like adoration, easy to read, a sudden shadow fell one day. Cornelia was the first to look up at the window and gasp with an instant premonition of evil. Miad's eyes followed hers and recognized at once the sinister silhouette of his enemy, the piglike Mr. Levis.

"That's nothing," he said as he returned hastily to his workbench. "Only Mr. Levis." But in spite of the reassuring words he felt a sinking of the heart. Instinctively he was sorry that Mr. Levis had caught him in the act of looking at his father. He shook out the duster he had lately used and, climbing on a trestle, draped the cloth over the window. "I guess I worked enough today," he muttered to Cornelia.

CHAPTER IX

On the following morning, just as Miad was about to descend to the cellar, Mr. Levis appeared at the shop. There was a sort of armed neutrality between the jewel smuggler and Mr. Crabbe. Mr. Levis's thick skin balanced exactly the astuteness of old man Crabbe, and each knew the intimate history of the other so thoroughly that any move made by either necessarily would have to start from scratch. Without ever having had the fact explicitly stated, Miad was aware that Crabbe despised Mr. Levis as fervently as Mr. Levis detested Mr. Crabbe, and that this mutual disregard acted like a malignant magnet between them. Consequently he was more interested than surprised when a series of

remarks and moves led the two men by gradations to the point of descending to the cellar.

Miad, ignored, stood aside to let them pass,
his brain active in an attempt to link Levis's
visit with the occurrence of the preceding
afternoon. What was Pig Eyes after? Had
the duster draped over the window aroused his
ferreting curiosity? Did he wish to make sure
that the body of John Blake was still in place?
If so, why? This reverie passed in a second
and ended with an illuminating flash totally
disconnected with the matter in mind. His
eyes had suddenly dilated to a stare of horror
as they caught a mere glimpse of a small object
in Crabbe's right hand.

For his own convenience in the art of taxidermy Mr. Crabbe had invented an instru-
ment that was a cross between a bradawl and
skewer. It had a strong stocky handle and a
long blade of rigid steel. At his workbench
it looked as commonplace and innocent as a
draftsman's lead pencil, but held like a weapon of offense, as he was holding it now, it

appeared totally strange and sinister to Miad's fascinated stare. He knew Mr. Crabbe to be a creature of habit, and it was his invariable habit to lay down whatever tools he was working with when he left his bench.

The old man descended the last few steps with silent and uncanny alacrity. Only the hard lump that sprang into Miad's throat prevented him from letting out a yell of warning. Something had told him, as loudly as though it had been shouted, that the long-bladed bradawl, vibrating in Mr. Crabbe's grip, was about to connect with Mr. Levis's oily person. Unable to cry out, he slithered down the stairs and arrived just as Mr. Levis, after a swift survey of the cellar, turned to face Mr. Crabbe, who stood with his hands at his back and slightly bent, as if he were slouching.

Miad was not deceived by the stooping posture. He knew that in reality his aged partner was as taut as a bowstring. Perceiving that by chance the long blade of the awl was thrust through one of the loops of the bowknot of the

thong which, acting as a belt, held up Mr.
Crabbe's apron, he reached out, caught the end
of the strip of leather and gave it a violent
pull. The noose closed, imprisoning the skew-
erlike blade. Mr. Crabbe emitted a grunt of
fury and tugged spasmodically. In vain. The
thong was not only strong; it gripped like
glue. Mr. Levis smiled. When he smiled his
overfull lips drew back until they showed a
gleam of sharp white teeth. He took from one
of his pockets a sheaf of stamped postal cards,
arranged them fanwise and held them out
toward Mr. Crabbe.

"Take one, you old pinhead," he snarled.
"Any one of the lot. It's like what I mail to
myself every time I come here."

Mr. Crabbe seemed to shrivel and turn limp,
becoming at once his usual self, the familiar
old man with steel-rimmed glasses pushed high
into his disheveled hair, whom Miad loved
without ever saying so and, for the matter of
that, without knowing it. Relinquishing the
handle of the imprisoned awl, he reached out

his right hand and took one of the cards. Upon perceiving that both the old man's hands were empty of any weapon, a look of surprise and doubt filled Mr. Levis's piglike eyes, but he made no comment. He pushed by Crabbe to the stairs, passed Miad, and departed. The two partners, man and boy, followed him presently with slow steps and pensive mien.

"Now, what was he after?" asked Miad of no one in particular.

"Why didn't you keep your hands offen me?" growled the old man testily. "Ain't I tired to death of having him pesterin' us?"

"Read that card, and I guess we'll know something," replied Miad.

Mr. Crabbe pulled down his glasses and spelled out the following: " 'Note postmark. This day I went to Crabbe's shop in Cobbled Court. It has two cellars.' "

"Don't that mean nothing to you, you old pigsticker?" asked Miad hotly, just beginning to realize the narrowness of the escape.

"Mean anything!" snapped Mr. Crabbe, unwilling to admit that Miad's timely interference had saved two men from sudden death, one by a swift thrust to the medulla oblongata and the other by hanging. "Mean anything? Of course it does. It means that pig of a Levis has been telling himself in the open mails about our two cellars. That's what it means."

"It means something else, too," said Miad, frowning. "I don't know just what, but it means something else."

He was right. That very afternoon, while he was industriously at work in the cellar, there came to him from above the dull thud of a falling tool. So many weeks had passed since last he had heard the signal that for a moment he doubted his ears; nevertheless, he decided to obey it. He laid aside his work and slipped just within the masked entrance of the underground passage to Hague Street. Presently he heard Crabbe's voice coming down the open stairway, querulous, unwontedly loud.

"Sure, I got the certificate. Everything's regular, I tell you. Nothing you can't see.

Nothing. Only awaiting burial." Before each phrase, a pause; in each pause the indistinct rumble of an unheard question. Thus: Rumble, and then, "Sure, I got the certificate." Rumble. "Everything's regular, I tell you." Rumble. "Nothing you can't see."

Again a lump rose into Miad's throat, a different kind of lump. Footsteps. They were coming down. First Mr. Crabbe came into the line of vision, and then an officious stranger. Not a truant officer, not a blue-coated cop, but patently officious, for all that.

"Is it this here, now?" asked the stranger with awe in his voice for the lifelike gleam that darted at him from beneath John Blake's half-fallen eyelids. He leaned over, raised a tag, grimy and discolored with age, and read the faded inscription, "Awaiting burial." Then he glanced at the certificate Mr. Crabbe had handed him and read the date, "Mch. 15, 1876." The stranger leaped back.

"Holy mackerel! Seven years! Of all the cheek! Seven mortal years awaiting burial!

You know the law, Mr. Crabbe. I reckon you'll hear more of this, but in the meantime I give you two days to show up at the Board of Health with a proper certificate of interment. Failing that, we'll give him a pauper's funeral come Wednesday. That's all I got to say, Mr. Crabbe, but it seems to me you're due for a fat fine when I report the facts."

He departed. Crabbe stood pinching his underlip and staring lugubriously at his too perfect handiwork in the art of embalming. There had been a time when he considered John Blake as an asset, his own individual property; but that day had long passed. It was years since he had accepted unconsciously and without a mental reservation Miad's assumption of undisputed proprietorship. Miad crept forth from hiding, white of cheek and of lip.

"They can't do it, can they, Crabbe? They can't take my father?"

"It's that pig-eyed Levis," replied the old man with well-meant indirectness. "They got the law on us, son." He threw up his head and tipped it to one side in a grotesque effort to appear casual. "What you say," he continued, as one who gives utterance to a brain wave, "we give your dad a fine, third-class funeral? Everything regular, with an honest-to-God hearse, two carriages and a tombstone?"

"Bury John Blake!" cried Miad aghast. "Crabbe you must be crazy."

"Crazy, is it?" snapped the old man. "I suppose perhaps you're going to take a cab, call on your lawyer, and draw up an injunction against the Board of Health!"

"Is that what I got to do?" asked Miad gravely, and started on a run for the stairs.

"Miad!" called old Crabbe loudly. "Miad, I was joking of you!" But Miad was gone.

The only lawyer Miad had ever heard of was the father of Harold Grimble, the schoolmate whom he had thrashed years ago for trying to kiss Cornelia by force. Within an hour he had discovered and burst into the privacy of

GREAT VAN SUTTART MYSTERY

Mr. Grimble's office. Within the next thirty minutes Mr. Grimble passed through the emotions of consternation, anger, interest, amusement, more consternation, awe and respect.

The youngster before him, blue-eyed, shock-headed, sturdy but small for his thirteen and a half years, desired the preposterous. In brief, he wished to enjoin the Board of Health of the City of New York against tampering with his unburied father. The last straw piled up to break the back of the lawyer's reluctance to undertake so bizarre a case was the production of a bank pass book from Miad's tattered pocket, accompanied by the announcement that he had three thousand dollars for the defense of John Blake.

Let us skip all tedious details. Assume the injunction against summary burial. Picture Miad Blake in a court of law at a hearing to show cause why the act of enjoinment should not be terminated. A hot day. Moist, murmuring voices, stating cold facts coldly. A fly bothering his honor, the judge. A small

hum of interest aroused by evidence as to the
extraordinary permanence of John Blake.
The said hum entirely drowned out as far as
the judge was concerned by the buzzing of the
fly. The judge's summing up, cut and dried,
wrapped in all the verbal mummy cloths of
the law, totally unintelligible to Miad and to
all others present, but instantly divined by
counsel through watching the left corner of the
judge's clean-shaven mouth. A faint stir of
conclusion. Mr. Grimble turns to Miad.

"Sorry, my boy."

Miad, clutching the back of the bench in
front of him and wagging his round head from
side to side as if striving to come up from the
bottom of the judge's sea of words into the
light. "Sorry? What do you mean?" People
stretching; the district attorney representing
the Board of Health gathering his papers preparatory to departure. Miad, almost whimp-
eringly to his counsel, Mr. Grimble, "Say,
what do you mean? You tell me quick what
he said."

"He said you would have to bury your father. In plain English, he confirmed the action of the Board of Health."

Miad, leaping to his feet and addressing the astonished bench: "Say, you, where you been? Ain't you heard nothing? You can't take John Blake, because he's mine, see? Nobody can take something what belongs to somebody else and if you should come around and look at him and let him look at you just once you would see gol-durned quick that you can't bury John Blake. It—it wouldn't be right. And anyway, he's mine, see? He's my father."

At first the judge's broad face reddened ominously, but as he perceived the exceedingly small size and genuine fervor of his assailant a Jovian calm settled on the magisterial brow, even though no gleam of intelligence lighted up the magisterial eye.

The judge in an unctuously benevolent voice: "Young man, none should be lacking in respect for the quality of filial affection which gave rise to your outburst, even when

expressed in terms that show little apprecia-
tion of the dignity of the court. Apparent
clashes between sentiment and justice are in-
evitable to the immature mind. It is evident
that by some treatment of the object of
injunction the normal process of decay has
been temporarily arrested. That fact, however, is irrelevant, if not distinctly dangerous
in general application. The court has no intention and no inclination to add one more to a
long list of questionable precedents. The point
of law, strangely enough, is one to which you
have given stress—namely, possession. It is
an ancient and established principle of both
spiritual and temporal precedure that, once
the essence of the personality has flown, possession of the body automatically ceases,
whether such possession be considered in its
actual or testamentary capacity."

"Say," interrupted Miad at this point, "are
you talking to me?"

"I am," stated the judge. In spite of himself a glint in his eye answered the twin glint

in Miad's, which was plainly asking for a fight and no favor. "I am trying to convey to you that while you live, your body is your own to develop, mutilate or destroy within certain bounds; but with death, your tenancy and possession cease simultaneously. Even had your father willed his remains in due form——"

"Aw, cut it out!" interrupted Miad again. "Talk to me straight. Do I keep John Blake or don't I?"

"No; you do not!" roared the judge, turning purple. "Clear the court!"

No one had to clear Miad from the premises. He dodged, he butted, he crawled and scampered.

By reason of his small size and great activity he was the first out from the building, and ten minutes later was in fervid consultation with Mike, friend and mucker-out of the Maclintock stables. The raw-boned stable hand was all too ready for any act of allegiance to the shock-headed, blue-eyed terror who gave life to the lawless independence of Cobbled

Court. He could not have put the feeling in words, but deep within him he knew that Miad was more than Miad. He was the incorporated spirit of revolt and indomitable grit, the kid who never turned his back on a fight. Nevertheless Mike was troubled.

"And after that, Miad?" he asked. "What about after that?"

"Never you mind after that," declared Miad stoutly, dismissing by an effort a flicker of doubt from his own eyes. "Let's get started."

The only horse in the stables was a fat pensioned dobbin; the only rig a dilapidated two-seated surrey with the top gone. Why struggle through the long underground passage that linked the cellar of Crabbe's shop with a house in Hague Street—that very house beneath which Miad as a baby of three had stood within his mother's encircling arms, seen her turn white—whiter than white—and heard her call "Run, darling, run!" with frenzied panic in her voice?

Miad, absorbed in trundling your father's

body, wake up! Think, Miad. What happened on that day of long ago? Two men peering down from the street through a rough hole, and your mother staring up at them, aghast, petrified with something above and beyond terror. You, scampering at your mother's command. And then—behind you—mist of descending sand. Trickle of pebbles. Rumble and thunder of caving rocks. Miad, did you never hear of the great Van Suttart mystery? Skinflint Van Suttart; William, his son; and Mary, William's wife—all wiped from the face of the earth as a wind that is passed? Look up the date, Miad.

But Miad was too intent upon the task in hand to gather up the threads of a mystery that centered in his small person alone out of all the millions in the city, and of which he had never so much as heard. From the age of three he had been a reservoir of such knowledge as would have flooded the front pages of all the press; but he did not know it. He might easily never know it. Here, in the cellar, gathered closely together for the first time by the measure of actual space, were five people whom fate in life had cruelly lashed to one another with underground feeler and taproot; Miad, himself; William Van Suttart; William's father; William's wife, who was also Miad Blake's mother; and, last, yet greatest of them all, John Blake, sometime porter, starting out on a pilgrimage away from the grave.

Through immemorial habit we like to associate pomp and circumstance with the moving of the dead. Here was no pomp or circumstance, yet I venture to assert that never in the history of human devotion was the husk of one beloved in life and treasured in death handled more reverently or with deeper consecration than was the body of John Blake on this urgent occasion. A hard job for a stable hand, however brawny, aided only by an undersized boy of thirteen. But don't forget that the boy was Miad. Laborious—yes, But let's skip all that.

Here we are, back at the beginning of the chapter, back in Hague Street, back at the door that opened outward, back to Mike, smelling strongly of the stables, tugging—and Miad, pushing—even while the agent of the Board of Health, stationed at the entrance to the shop in Cobbled Court, stuffed his pipe preparatory to another long, untroubled smoke.

In due course the box was placed in the surrey, facing forward, foot down, sharply tilted against the back seat and loosely draped with the checkered, red-and-white tablecloth. Miad climbed to the driver's place, took up the lines and stared before him, down the short length of Hague toward the rumble and crash of Pearl Street and the wide world. For a moment his small shoulders seemed to slump. He turned his head for a last word with the stable hand.

"If I don't come back, Mike, tell old Maclintock you sold the horse and rig to a ragman for a hundred dollars and keep the other fifty for yourself like I told you. If he gets awful mad I guess you'll just have to give him the fifty, too, like you was doing it out of your own wages. Tell him the ragman was in an awful hurry."

"Sure, Miad," grunted the stable hand, filled for some inexplicable reason with a blind rage that watered at the eyes. "Sure, that's all right, Miad. Don't you be worrying about me. But where you going? That's what I want to know. Where you going to take your dad to, Miad?"

"I don't know," said Miad. Then his shoulders suddenly braced, he slapped the fat dobbin's back with the reins and called back over his shoulder "But I'm going!"

At the time all this happened—namely, in the month of May, 1883—the Bowery was a far more colorful street than it is today. Gone are the secondhand clothing barkers who used to seize violently upon hayseeds as their natural prey. Gone are the docile hayseeds and their carpetbags. Gone are the pistols, which shone to boyish eyes with an effulgence that dimmed the pawned jewels amid which they nested. Gone the tradition that if you were the first customer to enter a pawnshop on a Monday morning the weeping broker would part with anything you coveted at next to nothing in cash rather than see you depart without making a purchase. Gone, too, the vivid stain of a string of dime museums, most astounding of all the fads and fancies of a pseudo-Victorian epoch.

"Step in! Step in! A dime does it. See the only one-eyed giant. Feel the fifth leg of a live calf. Hear the wild man of Borneo roar and the dog-faced boy howl. All for ten cents or a dime. The only speaking skeleton and the fattest woman in the world, side by side. Study the wonders of Nature. Witness the ravages of disease, done to the life in wax. Pull the bearded woman's whiskers. All for a dime. Step in for a dime."

CHAPTER X

EVEN so and notwithstanding, the spectacle of a very small boy driving an ancient surrey, staring straight ahead, slapping spasmodically the broad back of a very fat horse, and apparently totally unaware of the grotesque appearance of the box that loomed perilously against the inadequate back seat, was enough to make even the street which had winked knowingly during half a century at the pranks of P. T. Barnum and his great American Museum over on Broadway, take a long, long look and suddenly gasp furiously for air.

Betrayal! Stab in the back! Oh, treachery of the elements! Look around, Miad! See what the vagrant breeze has done to the fluttering, checkered, red-and-white shroud!

GREAT VAN SUTTART MYSTERY

Beholding the gaping, stricken, wide-eyed faces of the passers-by, Miad had no need to look around to see what they saw. These people were staring at John Blake himself, and John Blake undoubtedly was calmly staring back. Poor Miad! How his blood turned to ice in spite of the hot May sun! How he gulped at the biggest lump his throat had ever known! Alas! All was lost and he was beaten!

Unslapped, the fat horse came to a stop. A large round man was standing in the doorway of one of the many dime museums. He also stared, but with a difference. He darted with amazing deftness through the gathering crowd on the sidewalk and approached the gruesome yet pitiful cortège.

"Hello, Miad. What you got? Where you going?"

Miad came up slowly from the profundities of his despair. "Hello, Mr. Eckstrom," he murmured in a weak voice, Then suddenly, his eyes blazing with hope, "Say, Dutchy, I got one of the most wonderful works of Nature and old man Crabbe that you ever seen."

Three minutes later the crowd, laughing sheepishly at itself for being fooled, was rapidly dispersing while Mr. Eckstrom accepted the consignment of John Blake, deceased, neatly packed into a genuine mummy case, and called loudly to his barker for aid in removing the treasure to his museum. Miad had known better than to lie. He had gulped out the whole truth, won the showman as a stalwart ally against the law, and actually arranged to pay for lodging for his father. John Blake was to be placed inconspicuously and never to be barked among the attractions.

That matter attended to, Miad drove back disconsolately to Cobbled Court by a roundabout way, delivered horse and rig, received in return the money he had left with the stable hand, ignored the gnawing curiosity in Mike's questioning eyes, trampled viciously on the extended foot of the loafing agent of the Board of Health, and dodged past Crabbe's shop, up into the fastness of his own room. His father was gone. He, Miad, was alone!

"Gol-dast that rapscallion!" groaned the agent.

"Him!" grunted Mike without sympathy. "Why, he ain't no rapscallion. He's a wonder; that's what he is. You don't rightly know what a wonder that lad is. Perhaps you'll never find out; and then again, perhaps you will."

When the agent did begin to find out, which occurred at the moment when he lugged a straw mattress down to the cellar preparatory to making himself comfortable for the night, bedlam broke loose in Cobbled Court. Discovery of the abduction of John Blake and the arrest of Miad were practically simultaneous, since Miad had no chance to flee from his room, even had he wished. Mr. Crabbe was also taken into custody, but was as promptly released from the police station when he proved an alibi out of the mouth of the agent himself, who declared he had been in constant touch and conversation with the old man.

On the next morning Miad was haled before the selfsame judge with whom he had joined battle on the previous day. If he had looked as forlorn as his small size, broken-crowned hat and tattered clothes warranted, it is possible that the court would have laid aside its pomposity, gained a great deal of amusement, and, in the end, made a friend for life. But Miad himself did not look forlorn. Far from it. There was such a gleam in his eye as transcends the barrier of age and affirms that, whether all men are created equal or not, their battling souls certainly are, and that from the very day of birth.

With set lips the judge heard what should have been a diverting case. On the face of it, it appeared that the mummy of a full-grown man had been spirited from under the nose of the agent on guard by a boy thirteen and a half years old and four feet four inches tall. That was a palpable impossibility. It was highly probable, however, that with the aid of others the said boy had staged the vanishing act and could disclose the details. What could be simpler and easier than to put him on the stand and clear up at once the annoying mystery? Alas! In all the assembly of important grown-up people present there was not one with sense enough to call out "Low bridge, judge!" or "Stop, look and listen!" or "Beware of the dog!" or even "Cheese it, your honor!"

"Swear the prisoner."

"Prisoner?" asked Miad meekly. "What for? I ain't done nothing."

For a moment there was silence in the court room while the judge stared fixedly at Miad and Miad stared even more fixedly at the judge. Then again: "Swear the prisoner!"

Miad took his place in the dock and duly kissed the Book.

"Boy," said the judge in his most ponderous and impressive manner, "you are accused of conniving at the abduction of the mortal remains of one John Blake, said to have been your father. I charge you, by the solemn oath which you have taken, to tell the truth, the whole truth and nothing but the truth about this scandalous affair, undertaken in open contempt of the order of the court. Proceed."

"I don't know what you're talking about," declared Miad. "Nobody I ever seen talks like you do."

Titters. Rattle of the gavel. Order restored. The judge leans far forward toward the prisoner.

"Tell exactly how you stole the body of John Blake, who helped you, and what you did with it. You can understand that, can't you?"

"Two thousand years," murmured Miad. Then his wide-open eyes turned glassy and his lips set tightly in a straight line.

"What?" cried the judge. "What did you say? Repeat that."

The clerk, reading: "He said, 'Two thousand years,' your honor."

"Two thousand years? What do you mean?

GREAT VAN SUTTART MYSTERY

What does he mean by that? Speak up, boy!
What do you mean? Come on, now! What
do you mean?"

At the moment the judge first asked that
question the hands of the big clock on the wall
pointed to half past ten; when he asked it for
the last time they had crawled around to half
past twelve. It is impossible to depict in words
what happened to the men present, particularly to the judge, in the two hours of elapsed
time. In the face of Miad's cool immobility
they turned hot, sweated, grew old, forgot that
they were clerk, constable, magistrate or spec-
tator, turned desperate; in short, allied themselves in a blood pact, subconsciously aware
that the whole fabric of the complacent self-
respect of the grown-up people of the world
was in peril before the obduracy of a child.
An irresistible tradition had met the immovable and was gasping for its life.

How picture the judge? How describe his
ascent from routine dignity to Jovian wrath?
How cram the crash of his thunder into one

short paragraph—his sonorous maledictions, reverberations of the awfulness of the outraged law and threats of sentence for contempt of court? Wind. Nothing but wind. Hot air! But where words really and truly fail is in the sad task of depicting the honorable judge's trip, tumble and rumble down the steep stairs of Olympus, past the level of everyday propriety, and down, down into the cellar, nay, the very ash can of human deportment. Red-eyed. Blue-nosed with rage of the fishwife brand. Clothes and hair in disorder. Fist pounding. And, oh! the naughty word, asked of the world at large: "What in hell did he mean?"

At this point Miad broke his long silence for the first time, and that only in a manner of speaking. He addressed the crowd unofficially in the following aside: "Don't he look funny?"

A vast composite gasp. The immovable has yielded; not to the judge, but to the crowd! Silence has opened its mouth, spoken to the masses and crowned them above pompous authority. Swift whirl of the wheel of allegiance. Another gasp; and then ripple, rumble and roar of laughter. The crowd, all of it, is uproariously for Miad. Furious pounding of the gavel. "Order! Order! Clear the court! Constable—agent—take him away! Get the truth out of him, do you hear me? Get the truth if you have to wring his stubborn little neck. Take him away! Clear the court!"

Could any scene be funnier than the highly illegal trial of Miad Blake, culminating in his removal between a huge policeman on one side and the rapidly aging representative of the Board of Health of the city of New York on the other? Behold him! Four feet four, sturdy as they make them in that size, eyes staring calmly from a petrified face, marching along to Police Headquarters with his small grimy hands held within the paws of two large and exceedingly foolish-looking men.

Yes; one thing could be funnier. At five

o'clock of that same day, Mike, the stable hand, entered the shop in Cobbled Court and addressed old man Crabbe in the following manner:

"Say, Crabbe, you had ought to take a walk around to Headquarters and buy your way in with a five-dollar bill. They got Miad sitting on the desk just like he used to sit on this here bench. I never seen him look so small, not even then. They's six cops, two sergeants and the captain, all with their coats off. Them as has quit sweating is oozing blood from the mouth and ears. They sure need sympathy and aid."

"What they trying to do with him?" asked Mr. Crabbe, laying down his tools and pushing his steel-rimmed glasses high on his forehead.

"They're trying to make him tell what he done with his dad."

"Trying to make Miad tell!"

Then the funnier thing happened. Mr. Crabbe's rawhide length began to twist from the feet up like a revolving corkscrew. His knees rapped against each other with a bony sound. His small stomach went in and out like a bellows in action. His narrow chest performed the same convulsion, but with a slightly different beat, thus suggesting syncopated time. His lips and eyes worked in and out, giving to his wrinkled face the horrible expression of a dying dogfish. A spluttering sound issued from his mouth.

"Say, what are you doing of?" demanded the stable hand, aghast.

"I'm laughing," choked Mr. Crabbe. "Laughing of myself to death!"

Miad passed the night in solitary confinement, and on the following day, without reappearing in court, was testily sentenced to the mercies of the Cherry Society. Hand in hand with Terry Dugan, the patrolman of his district, he started out for the dreaded refuge of the orphaned young. At the risk of bringing a blush of shame to the composite face of the entire police force of New York, let it be recorded as a matter of history that Officer

JOHN BLAKE MAKES A STOP-OVER

Terence Dugan wore a squashy cap with a visor; a wrinkled belted coat of blue, and a complete circle of eye-brows, burnsides and whiskers, out of which peered his hairless eyes, nose and mouth. On his hip he carried a blackjack and inside his breast a heart.

As he walked along, holding Miad firmly by the hand, he was plunged in a sad reverie. He was wondering what his beat would be like, once the flash of Miad's eyes, legs and wit were gone from the environs of Cobbled Court, and once Pearl, Frankfort, Vandewater and New Chambers streets should no longer be a quivering center of electrical disturbance echoing to Miad's irreverent cry of "Hey! Terry! Come out from behind them bushes." And then, in tones of assumed terror, "Hi! fellers! Cheese it. Cheese it, the cop!"

Breaking into the reverie came Miad's voice, startlingly meek: "Say, Terry, what is this here Cherry Society you're taking me to?"

"Awful, Miad. Most as awful as a hospital."

GREAT VAN SUTTART MYSTERY

Miad sighed. As they were entering the juncture of Pearl with the New Bowery a fine team of truck horses hitched to an empty dray came jangling up Vandewater at a full trot, making a terrible clatter. Miad screwed his head around as the rattle approached. Nearer and nearer it came. Suddenly his eyes lighted to a belligerent gleam. When the noise was at its loudest he yelled at the top of his voice, "Runaway, Terry!"

In one swift heroic movement Officer Terence Dugan let go his prisoner, hurled himself at the bridles of the astonished, well-mannered horses and forced them back on their haunches. The patter of Miad's feet as he scampered down Vandewater Street was completely drowned out by the torrent of vituperation that poured from the infuriated teamster's mouth, only to die with a gurgling gulp as Terry explained to him that if his team had not been running away then he, Terence Dugan, would be hard put to it to explain the escape of his prisoner, Miad Blake.

JOHN BLAKE MAKES A STOP-OVER

"Miad! You was arresting of Miad, Terry?" asked the truckman, grinning broadly with comprehension. "Well, climb aboard and I'll drive you around to the police station and tell 'em about you being a hero."

Needless to say, Miad asked no further start on the arm of the law than to reach the entrance to Maclintock's warehouse in Vandewater Street. He passed through to Cobbled Court and went into definite retirement. No one was going to trap him in his room again. He slept in the stables, in the rubbish heaps of the alley or near the door in the Hague Street house, and by day worked in the cellars. For some time minions of the court and of the Board of Health troubled his haunts in half-hearted fashion, but finally Mike passed along word to him that no officer dared take the risk of haling him before the judge again. *Ex cathedra,* the judge wanted Miad; unofficially, Miad was the last human being, born since Adam, whom he wished to see.

In the meantime Mr. Levis had not been

idle. Through his own snooping propensities he had unearthed the information that something very like the mummy of John Blake had been observed with consternation and final mirth riding up the Bowery in the back seat of a ramshackle surrey and had found sanctuary in one of the string of dime museums.

However, the wireless of the present has nothing on the system of communication of the underworld of yesterday. By the time the raiders reached and serched Eckstrom's establishment not only had the mummy again vanished; its very memory had been blotted from the communal mind of Eckstrom, his helpers and the entire street. If you want a visual demonstration of the definition of the familiar phrase "conspiracy of silence," send your wife down to the regions that surround Cobbled Court, follow her, ask anyone which way she went.

Of these developments Miad remained totally unaware for a period of several days; in fact, two weeks elapsed before he dared take the risk of entering Eckstrom's popular place of business. He dodged unnoticed through the throng of gaping patrons. Hurriedly he sought out the proprietor.

"Hey! Dutchy, what you done with him?"

The showman looked at Miad's troubled face long and thoughtfully. "It was this way," he said finally. "A friend on the job tells me they were raiding all the dime dumps for your dad, see? So this is what I done, Miad; I shipped him on a whaler as Madeira wine for a two-year trip around the Horn and back. I guess that will fix 'em, eh, Miad? By the time he gets back nobody won't remember nothing. Ain't I done right, Miad?"

Miad's heart was too full for words. He gulped and made hastily for the street and the solitude that is to be found in hurrying crowds. For weeks he haunted the wharves at the foot of the Old Slip, where high-headed sailing ships in large numbers still dragged heavily on their hawsers, battered, dejected, waiting to go and come no more, as if already they knew themselves for the white-winged ghosts of to-morrow.

Once or twice Cornelia, troubled and silent, accompanied him. She was just approaching the threshold to adolescence. Her spindling legs were beginning to take shape, as was her slim body. Her big black eyes, pale cheeks, and the curl in her tresses were whispering of beauty to come, and her heart was awaking to a lifelong mission of comfort. In other words, she was about to bud.

"Miad, how can we watch for the ship if we don't know its name?"

"Gee, Corny, you make me sick. Why, this ship won't be back for two years."

Then, on another day, "Miad, you make that Mr. Eckstrom tell you the ship's name. Do you hear? Come on with me now. You make him tell you, like I said."

Mr. Eckstrom put them off; he had forgotten; he would have to look it up; he had mislaid the bill of lading. No; it wasn't lost. Oh, no; he was sure of it. It would turn up.

Wait and see. It was sure to turn up. Thus at intervals for several months, during which Miad grew sadder and sadder, and Cornelia more and more troubled for him in her heart. At last came a day when with ponderous archness the fat Mr. Eckstrom—whom Miad had long since found to be dry to the touch—drew from his waistcoat pocket two blue slips of pasteboard.

"Here, take your girl to a show, Miad."

"She ain't my girl," muttered Miad. "She's just Cornelia, and you can keep your old tickets."

Dutchy's round face grew serious. He reached out, seized Miad by the scruff of the neck, thrust the tickets into his trouser's pocket and pushed him out into the street. "That's right. Lie about it. Why, Miad, I would be proud to have a girl like that. You do what I say now. Take her to the show, and mind you see everything."

The two children walked away listlessly, but finally Cornelia asked to see the tickets. "Eden

Musée," she read. Deftly she piloted Miad toward the address printed on them and, when they came to the entrance to the famous wax-works, gave up the tickets and marched him in. Immediately their eyes were riveted on one startling wonder after another. They felt a glow of gratitude toward Mr. Eckstrom—perhaps he wasn't so heartless after all. Distinguished Personages. Notorious Criminals. The Crowned Heads of Europe. Murder groups. Oh! Oh! Murders, done to the life!

Cornelia smiled up ingratiatingly at a big policeman. He did not smile back; not a flicker. She touched him. Oh! He was made of wax. They wandered farther. She came upon another stolid policeman and with a surreptitious flick of her heel kicked him on the shin. He said, "Ouch! What are you doing of?" and glared at her.

"Oh, please," she murmured, aghast, seizing Miad's arm with both her hands. "I thought you were wax. Truly I did. Please forgive me."

JOHN BLAKE MAKES A STOP-OVER

"Sure, kid," grunted the officer out of the corner of his mouth. "Don't you worry your little noddle. I like it. Sometimes they kicks, but mostly they pinches."

Deeper and deeper into the maze of wonders penetrated the two children until in a far obscure corner they came to a petrified stop, their eyes glued before them on an object, long familiar, but now glorified, transcended, promoted to a place among the immortals, preserved to fame in wax. And yet, itself was not of wax. No! Miad's breast heaved. A lump came into his throat. He tried to swallow it as of old, but in vain. It rose. It came out through his wide belligerent eyes and gushed down his cheeks in the form of shameless tears.

Cornelia took out her hankerchief, just such a handkerchief as the one with which she had wiped the blood out of his ear years, years ago when he had fought Harold Grimble for trying to kiss her against her will. With it she dried his eyes and mopped his cheeks while, just as at that other time, he never moved from his fixed position.

"Oh, Miad, my dear, dear boy, don't cry! They'll see you. Please don't cry, Miad dear!"

"It's my father," gulped Miad out of the profundities of an overwhelming joy. "My own father, John Blake."

CHAPTER XI

AN EVENT OF TRANSCENDENT IMPORTANCE

BETWEEN the years 1886 and 1890 an event of transcendent importance took place jointly in the city of New York and the village of Barmingdale, in the state of Connecticut. That the said event has never before been mentioned in print detracts nothing from its significance. Far from it. If anything, the omission adds allure to the occurrence. Why? To save space and time, let the answer be packed into another question. Can you think of publicity and dried rose leaves at one and the same time without a jolt? Can you? Here is the event, recorded in exactly half a dozen words: Cornelia Van Suttart budded into womanhood.

GREAT VAN SUTTART MYSTERY

It is conceivable that some will carp at the above paragraph, considering it a species of hoax. Let all such substitute for the phrase "an event of transcendent importance" the word "miracle." If the turning of water into wine is conceded to be miraculous, how much more so the metamorphosis of Cornelia! Yesterday, all spindling legs, thin arms, thin chest, pale cheeks, dropped eyelids and two long pigtails; in short, a bit of loose-jointed animation to which men were wont lightly to call out, "Hey, kid! Watch your step or something will snap!"

But today—ah, today! Oh, the lift of her chin and neck, the proud burden of her glossy hair, the petal tints beneath her breathing pallor, the slim roundness of her blue-eyed beauty, striding along, sublimely unconscious, a dream. within a dream. Catch your breath. Groan. Send up your silent prayer: "How I wish I knew that girl!" Swift-fingered Time did it, and has since done it to another generation; but if you should meet Cornelia even in this youngster year of 1925, dried rose leaves would recall the rose.

Life is full of injustices, and it seems peculiarly unfair that Miad Blake, who at the age of eight years and five months had fought Harold Grimble for attempting to kiss Cornelia forcibly and had been her matter-of-fact champion ever since, should have been deprived by circumstances of the joy of witnessing her blooming. Soon after the day when the two as children had discovered the lost, strayed or stolen remains of the perpetuated John Blake, established as within a hall of fame amid the waxworks of the renowned Eden Musée, Cornelia had been removed from the plebeian atmosphere of Public School No. 112. She had gone away; far, far away from Roosevelt Street and the ken of Miad Blake.

The removal marked a long divergence in their orbits from the point of their conjunction at one and the same school back in the nebulous days of childhood. Miad's feet continued in the path in which they were set from the moment when his honesty blew up a highly lucrative and illicit business and left behind only cordwood and bucksaw, immemorial emblems of the sweat of the human brow.

It was a laborious, lonely and secluded path, enlivened only by the taciturn presence of old man Crabbe, who was growing very old indeed, and by occasional escapes from the confines and environs of Cobbled Court to pay a respectful visit to his embalmed father, John Blake. Cornelia, playmate and ally, was gone to a place called Barmingdale, beyond the confines of the known world of Cobbled Court.

Evidence as to what Barmingdale happens to be doing today is not at hand, but what it did to previous generations is on record in many of the sweetest drawing-rooms and at many of the coziest afternoon tea tables of the civilized world.

If you meet a woman from fifty to ninety years old and are in doubt as to which—a woman whose serenity is peppered with wit, whose manners are both easy and restrained and whose mind is as daring as her standards are secure—interrupt; say, "Pardon me, madam, but when were you at Barmingdale?" She will flush a delicate shell pink—such a pale pink as is rapidly going out of fashion—her eyes will twinkle, and to your surprise and confusion she will rap out the exact date.

Figuratively speaking, it was as long a cry from East Broadway and the public school in Roosevelt Street to Barmingdale in 1886 as it was from a ranch in Montana or from the governess' room in the White House in Washington, and yet various little girls made the various journeys to a single end successfully, among them Cornelia. Considering the extreme simplicity, not to say skimpiness, of her clothing and the nonexistence of her pin money between the ages of seven and fourteen, this assertion calls for elucidation.

Cornelia had been born and lived all her life in a house on the corner of East Broadway and Market Street, a corner wiped out when Manhattan Bridge was built. The house had three

stories, a high stoop of stone steps within rail-
ings of scrolled ironwork, a broad front door
flanked by black pilasters and surmounted by
an enormous fanlight, an old-fashioned bell
pull and worn doormat from which the word
"Welcome" had been omitted. A queer way
to describe a house, all from across the street;
but, strange to say, very few people were in
a position to picture it any more intimately
during the years of Cornelia's childhood. She
herself could not remember when three people
—the elder Van Suttart, William Van Suttart,
his son, and her own mother, Mary Malone
Van Suttart—vanished from its doorway
one day, never again to enter, and Mr.
Prosper Frete, accompanied by his sister, came
in.

Go back in your mind, away back to the
troubled years immediately succeeding the
Civil War. Forget for a moment the gloomy
abode in East Broadway and enter the no less
gloomy counting-house and warerooms of the
ancient firm of Hendricks, Jacob Hendricks,

AN EVENT OF IMPORTANCE

Van Suttart and Partners, on Front Street. Remember that all the Hendrickses were long dead and that the old skin-flint, the elder Van Suttart, was virtually the whole works, except for a single silent partner, Prosper Frete by name.

Consider the consternation when the Van Suttarts, father and son, failed to come back from their noontime dinner. Never—never in the long history of the firm—had such an unheralded absence occurred. Picture the sending of a messenger, posthaste, to the dwelling in East Broadway. Consternation heaped on consternation! The dinner untouched upon the table, the cook distracted, a baby crying—crying for the mother who was never again to come—and that baby no other than Cornelia.

Now turn your mind from Cornelia, weeping in her crib, to consideration of the person of Prosper Frete. To look at him would tell you no more than a glance at the outside of the sombre house in East Broadway. He was a sallow young man with sleek black hair and eyes of a pale, yellowish green. That is all you would see, but here are the inside facts: He had paid two hundred dollars for a substitute in the Civil War and, in everything but outward appearance, he was the unrecognizable, commonplace, everyday continuation of the caricature immortalized under the name of Uriah Heep. In other words, he was born with an old heart in one of those smooth, young-looking bodies which never seem to wither.

Mr. Frete knew a sure thing and the right move even before he saw them; and that is saying a great deal, for he was gifted with the foresight of a vulture and the cunning premonition of a weasel waiting for a hen to lay an egg. But do not let your imagination run away with you. He was neither so repulsive nor so obvious as his famous prototype. To his business associates he was a man of his word, of meticulous manners in spite of a cold exterior, and of a sure and tenacious grasp of affairs; a man to be respected, perhaps to be feared, but in no way out of the ordinary in appearance.

To Cornelia, as far back as she could remember, he was merely one of a world of dark shadows. He was like the chairs, the pictures and the unchanging carpets and hangings of the gloomy house in East Broadway, only he moved, he came and went with the rhythmic regularity of a swinging pendulum. Even his sister, Miss Amantha Frete, was slightly more real, although almost as wordless. She had tiny, deep-set eyes and a thin face which ran all to a single point at the tip of her long nose, making her resemble one of Mr. Crabbe's short-handled bradawls.

In due course the cook who had been so distracted on the day of the vanishing of the entire Van Suttart family, barring the baby Cornelia, passed away. She had not been one of the shadows. Cornelia recollected her as a vague, indefinable blotch of light—a pale moon striving to break through the mist of childhood's clouds. The cook had had something to tell. Indeed, she had told it over and over again, only Cornelia could not remember it all. When she thought of the cook her brows would gather in a puzzled frown, but, try as she might, nothing more would come to mind beyond the oft-repeated admonition, "Believe me, my lone darling, your dear mother would never have left her baby of her own free will."

For many years after the good cook died Cornelia pondered over the hidden meaning in these words and finally was rewarded by a great light. The revelation came about in the following manner: School age and surreptitious wanderings in company with her playmate, Miad Blake, had made her familiar with many things, incidentally with the numerous pawnshops of the Bowery. Drawn by the fascination of their windows, she gradually absorbed their purpose. Here people, hard-pressed, gave up their treasures for money. Had not the cook called her, over and over, a loan darling? Presto! Her parents had left

her in pawn with the Fretes, against her dear
mother's will!

Absurd? Not at all. Nothing but the in-
cipient workings of an intelligent and logically
sound mind, leading to just such a sane yet
laughable conclusion as lurks in the memory
of every one of us. Whose youth has not confounded "God's free grace" with Godfrey's
Grace, or looked in vain for the colored ser-
geant? Be that as it may, Cornelia grew up
in the belief that she was a loan child, and as
a consequence was on her guard from babyhood to mind her p's and q's. Thus she herself
became one of the three shadows which flitted
in and out of the gloom of the house in East
Broadway. Only three, for subsequent to the
death of the cook Miss Frete undertook the
entire housework.

So quiet and docile was Cornelia as a little
girl that it is doubtful if anyone could have
thought of ways to subject her to persecution,
but, as it happens, there was no intent to abuse
her. She was simply left to her own meager

devices in a household that was by no means parsimonious, in spite of the inexplicably arduous labors of its mistress. The food was of the best that money could buy, and so were the materials in which Cornelia was clothed. If her appearance was skimpy and forlorn it was due to the shortcomings of Miss Frete's hasty and inexpert needlework.

Nevertheless and notwithstanding, can you imagine a stranger childhood? Cornelia, returning from school, jerks the bell pull. Miss Frete in apron and mobcap opens the door. No word is spoken. Cornelia goes to her room on the third floor, lays away her books and bonnet, and returns to help Miss Frete. No word is spoken.

The first floor, all but one room, is immaculately dusted daily, in silence. There is the wide hall of entrance, narrowing by half where the stairs go up. On the right of the hall, three large rooms, en suite; in front, the sitting room with windows on East Broadway; in the middle, the dining room, lighted by a single win-

AN EVENT OF IMPORTANCE

dow on Market Street and connected with the kitchen below by a huge dumb-waiter, large enough to handle logs of wood for the open fires. At the back, a room which Cornelia has rarely glimpsed through the crack of great sliding doors, perennially closed except for the swift, smooth passage of Mr. Frete in and out. By the shelves upon shelves of books, centering on a large flat desk, a reading lamp and a deep worn chair, Cornelia knows it to be a library.

After supper the three shadows gather for a time in the sitting room. No word is spoken. Cornelia studies her lessons. Once in a while, with an instantaneous lift of her long lashes, she seizes the vision of the two Fretes, male and female, and then, holding it within her hidden eyes, ponders upon it. They are silent, yet in communion. Miss Frete, sallow-faced, black-haired, smoothly sleek, pale-eyed. No word is spoken, yet Cornelia feels that these two commune. She dares not interrupt; she is too young to surmise.

Hold your breath, little girl, while pale eye says to pale eye, "All is well; all will be well. Silence, for I know what you are thinking. Silence, and let the mills of the gods grind for us." Then, always quite suddenly, Mr. Frete arises and passes through the dining room into the library, noiselessly closing the sliding doors behind him. No word has been spoken.

Apparently his green-yellow eyes never saw Cornelia at all—that is, never until a certain day when at the age of fifteen the surging life in her healthy little body sent her flying down the stairs into the front hall with such momentum that she could not stop at seeing the street door open to Mr. Frete's latchkey and swing wide. Giddy with the effort to halt her mad career, she went whirling into his arms. He caught her with characteristically quick decision, even before his mind yielded to a natural feeling of surprise.

The instant during which he held her close was sufficient to awaken him to a totally different sort of surprise. He stood her away from

him and swept his eyes up and down her person
with a sudden, seeing concentration which
brought a stain of blood to the pallor of her
cheeks. She dropped her eyelids and drew a
long quivering breath. She felt terribly
ashamed under his deliberate inspection and
thought it was because Mr. Frete had discovered her in the reprehensible act of flying down
the stairs. Presently he began to speak and
she was amazed at the fullness of the tones of
his voice and at the ease with which the silence
of years expressed itself.

"Cornelia," he said, "I have been so engaged with affairs that you have stolen a
march on me and grown into a big girl without
my knowing it. That dress is too tight, my
dear, and the skirt is too short. You have ac-
quired an ankle for which the decree of fashion
demands a more discreet veil, and soon your
braids must be piled upon your head. This
house has become, for a time, too small a place
to contain you."

At those words Cornelia felt a shiver of

dread. Was she not but a loan child? Had she by a single act of exuberant indiscretion forfeited her right to asylum in that house? If she were driven from it, where would she go? What could she do? Would it avail to plead with Mr. Frete? She raised her head and opened her deep eyes of Irish blue. He stared into them with what seemed an answering quiver of his whole frame, but before she could find words with which to plead he smiled and continued:

"You must go away to a genteel academy, the finest in the land. I shall speak to Amantha and instruct her to see that you are supplied with frocks bought at the stores and with all such things as the young ladies of a select school may require. In the meantime, will you avoid running unattended about the streets? I ask it as a personal favor to myself."

CHAPTER XII

SCHOOLDAYS—OH, THOSE SCHOOLDAYS!

OH, adolescence! Oh, breath of summer air!
Oh, clothes, new clothes, bandbox in the lap,
and trunks to follow; and girls, new girls,
strange girls, all atop of the ancient, the insti-
tutional Barmingdale stagecoach! Memory,
help me. Tradition, come to my aid. Time,
hold steady thy pellucid crystal globe. Behold the broad village way; the flaring, the
pantaletted Connecticut elms; the sweet white
church, green shuttered, pointing to God with
its slim aspiring steeple; and, at last, the old
school of ruddy red brick, nestling amid lawns,
fronds and matted creepers. But not so fast!
Houses—New England houses—all white and
piped with green. Drop two girls here and
three girls there.

A pleasing picture, but not enough. Open,

pellucid crystal. Disgorge. That's better. Look! In each of the houses, virginal rooms, candle-lighted, all converging to a single point of a Saturday night, and at that point, in the geometrical center of the various commodious kitchens, a tub—a large, shallow, oaken tub! Whence and what for? Baths, my masters. The weekly bath, nothing less! Yes, sir. Up to and including the last of the '80's, all those girls, pink cheeked, blue, brown, black and hazel eyed, used to— But what's that? A screen? Right again. At this point in the narrative the cook or old Marge used to put up a high, solid, three-leaved screen, impenetrable to the most searching gaze.

What other things can we see or hear during the three years Cornelia spent at Barmingdale? Well, here's a glimpse or two. Tiny Miss Petteril, very old, with twinkling eyes of jet, entering any class at any time and subjecting the girls to General X, a course in such intelligence as is commonly known among men as horse sense. The same pupils scurrying

around in tam-o'-shanters, inverness cloaks
and flopping unhooked galoshes. Fact. They
started that pseudo-modern fashion fully forty
years ago. Four desserts only in the way of
sweets brightened the scholastic term: Indian
pudding; ice cream; molded blocks of blanc-
mange, known as tombstones; and apple
dumplings, familiarly called baby heads.

Can you picture the way all those bright-
eyed girls used to bloom in the warm spring,
out of cloaks into clinging frocks of white?
See them marching to church, two by two—
this one mischievous, that one demure; this
one pious as a canary swelling with song on a
bright day, that one sweetly grave with the
thoughts she could not understand. Can you
wonder that the intellectual and artistic lions
of those times loved to go to Barmingdale?
Behold John Fiske, enormous, fat—but dry
to the touch—sitting in pontifical majesty to
deliver his famous lecture on American history. See him pause after the applause at the
end and glance at Mrs. Dimock almost plead-

ingly. Hear her say, "And now, Mr. Fiske, won't you kindly sing for us?"

A flutter—a tremor rustles across the hall. Good-by, old lecture; the truly awaited moment has arrived.

Can Mr. Fiske sing? He cannot, but he loves to. He squares his shoulders, lifts his leonine head, opens his mouth and roars, first in one favorite key and then in another, one song after another, each song three keys. Presently Mrs. Dimock gives an expert exhibition of tact. Can she stop him without hurting his dear feelings? No; never. Yes. No. Yes. She does. Strange to say, the girls have not laughed; not once. They file out with half-smiling, half-startled eyes, and gory thrills running up and down their backs as though they had been to a bull fight.

But Mr. Fiske was not the only one who sang to those girls in those times. Not by a jugful. Listen. While Cornelia Van Suttart was at Barmingdale there were three Junes, and in each June a full moon. Does that mean anything to you? No; nor to anyone of the modern generations of the students of Yale. Step in, sophisticated youth, license and the motor car; farewell, romance. But in Cornelia's day, with the full moon of June, up from the station came the Barmingdale stage-coach, loaded to overflowing with the glee club from New Haven.

Just how far the boys could go and just what the girls could do was set down between the solid walls of an ancient tradition. The boys might stand beneath the trees while the girls filed by to church. On coming out, the girls could walk to the marker elm, turn and come back. Thus the boys got three good, hungry, custom-sanctioned, long looks at the pretty faces from close quarters. They were not supposed to whisper—oh! no, never—and they always did.

Cornelia of course expected no one to whisper to her. The first time she passed before the line of eager eyes she even felt lonely, and then, the second time——

GREAT VAN SUTTART MYSTERY

"Cornelia! Cornelia Van Suttart!"

Her eyelids fluttered. Her heart came thumping into her throat. Up, up with her curling lashes. Lo! a flash of her hidden eyes of Irish blue. Just a glance, and down again. What a nice-looking boy, so tall, so gay, such pleased though startled eyes, such laughing lips! Who was he? Who could he be? Whence that voice, whispering her own name? Back, Cornelia, go back in memory. Further; still further. No! Yes! That nasty—that nice Harold Grimble who had tried to kiss her against her will long many years ago! That Harold Grimble whom Miad had licked but who had bloodied Miad's ear so that she had had to clean it with her own pocket handkerchief! No other! In justice she must snub the horrid boy.

The long line of girls turns for the final passing. Cornelia does not look up; she does not need to. Under the trees, an eddy of delicious warmth, an effulgence felt but yet unseen, an aura, a magnet, a brush of summer breezes drawing blood to paint a maiden's fleeting blush. As though that betrayal were not enough, at the exact moment of the closest conjunction of two palpitating planets of youth, Cornelia's lips, throat and voice deal her pride and sensibility a stunning blow. To her confusion and amazement she hears herself murmur, "Hello, Harold."

On the night of the concert—after the concert—hurry back to the Carolton House. Gleam of old mahogany furniture, never moved in a hundred years. Glow of involuted drugget rugs and rag carpets, all the colors of Joseph's coat. Shining, slim banister. Seize it; run up the stairs and into the room where flowers lie heaped upon the beds, the chairs, the floor. Stand and wait. Sit and wait. Stand again. Midnight at last. The tinkle of guitars and banjos, tuning up. Push the other girls aside. Snatch back the dimity curtain. Drop a flower. Throw a handful. Fill a pillow slip with fragrant blooms and send them out in a pelting shower! Then— Hark!

Listen—hand on fluttering breast. Harold's clear tenor voice, true as a bell, singing the song of songs of the day for that window alone:

> *"Thou art my true love, believe me;*
> *Promise thou ne'er wilt deceive me——"*

In three years there are only three Junes; in three Junes there are only three moons at the full; and that was all that Harold Grimble got of Cornelia or Cornelia of Harold while she was at Barmingdale. Nevertheless it was only that you might share in the palpitating events of those three widely spaced moonlit nights that you have been dragged all the way from Miad Blake and Cobbled Court, Mr. Frete and East Broaway, to a village in Connecticut. Come back. Leave behind those lovely girls and that bracing air, just as Cornelia had to do, not once, but three separate times.

The first time she did not know what to make of Mr. Frete and his sister, Amantha. They were mysteriously changed. Amantha still did all the work of the house, but with such miraculous expedition that she was free to accompany Cornelia every time she went into the streets. Mr. Frete was no longer a silent shadow. He talked as freely as on the day when Cornelia had plunged down the stairs into his arms. The words he used began to give him shape, so that gradually he became a presence. During the summer she gathered certain outstanding impressions. One was that she was never left alone except when in the privacy of her own room; another, that she was denied no whim save freedom; a third, that Mr. Frete, stepping out from shadow land, seemed not to have aged by a day in all her years of memory of him.

Naturally Cornelia longed to run over to Cobbled Court for a visit with Miad, and dreamed of running into Harold Grimble on the way. Young girls are quick to dream such things, and slow to put them in action. They are strange creatures. They seem to live in a daze that appears to get a sharper pleasure from awaiting an event than from forcing it. They like to have love and other things call for them. Just as naturally Cornelia ascribed Mr. Frete's increasing attention and the solicitude which prevented her from going out alone to the fact that she was growing up and was even now one of the Barmingdale young ladies.

Thus the first summer slipped by with amazing swiftness, leaving behind it a feeling of surprised emptiness, which was in turn rapidly swallowed by the excitement of returning to school. Without knowing how or why, Cornelia's inward hunger sensed that something was wrong, and when the second June full moon came along she took pains to give Harold Grimble such a look beneath the elms as a man never forgets to his dying day—one of those looks that pass along from a girl's sixteenth summer to a boy's nineteenth, strike deep their barbs and hang on as long as lingers the memory of breathless youth.

In vain. No sooner did she return to East

Broadway than Mr. Frete moved to the Metropolitan Hotel, while Cornelia was dispatched in the care of the silent Amantha to a watering place that was wholly uninteresting and unpeopled, since the look she had given Harold was not quite potent enough to guide him to her. Instead came Mr. Frete, every week-end, and took her for long walks on the sands. Gradually, so gradually that she could not mark the gradations of the change in him, he moved back into her world and became a live human being. She thought it was because she was growing up.

There came a day when she forgot all about being a loan child and asked him boldly for news of her parents. What were they? Who were they? What had become of them? A faint smile as of propitiation broke the curve of Mr. Frete's too full lips, and his pale eyes seemed to her to assume a benign look. They were sitting side by side on a broad flat rock. He laid his hand over hers and pressed it firmly.

"Listen, my dear," he said. "I do not wish
for a moment to blacken the memory of your
father and mother. Enough that they hurt
me, Prosper Frete, almost as deeply as they
wronged you when they went away. You will
never know the magnitude of the burden their
action cast upon my shoulders. Fortunately
I was a young man—a very young man for
such a responsibility. I slaved. I saved the
honor of the old Van Suttart name. But that
was not enough. There was you to think of,
an infant, a baby still in arms."

He paused, and in the silence the lapping
waves seemed to murmur, over and over again
in moist echo of the good cook's words, "Believe me, my lone darling, your dear mother
would never have left her baby of her own free
will!"

"I do not wish you to think of me and
Amantha as foster parents," resumed Mr.
Frete's resonant voice. "Never that, my dear.
Anything but that. Think of me as of one
who has never considered you a burden, even

in the most trying days. Regard me as one who welcomes you into womanhood without a thought of obligation on either side. The years will soon make us equals. Let us enter them not as ward and indulgent guardian, but as friends."

Hold it not against Cornelia that her ears were deafened by these words to the lapping echo of the good cook's oft-repeated saying. Remember her plastic youth, and measure the effect on a young girl of that phrase, "Regard me as one who welcomes you into womanhood." See the sweet gravity of her face deepen as she gently draws her hand away in the first conscious act of womanly reserve, and judge her not if, during her last year at school, the shining vision of Harold Grimble was sometimes dimmed by intruding thoughts of the goodness of Mr. Frete and of the great debt she owed him. At times she even made a calculation: Mr. Frete, at the least, though he did not look it, must be forty-two years old.

Here is another fact of transcendent importance: at the moment when Cornelia returned from her last term at Barmingdale and entered the sombre house in East Broadway, Miad Blake was in Mr. Frete's library of that very house, but the great sliding doors were tightly closed, as were Miad's thin lips.

There are some people who change so completely in the course of a few years that they become strangers to their own pasts; but not so Miad. To look at his sturdy chunk of a body, belligerent eyes and ungovernable hair was to behold the selfsame perky atom of humanity which at the age of three had taken the withered heart of old man Crabbe by assault and established a right in fee simple to every nook and cranny of Cobbled Court and its environs.

That being the case, what on earth was he doing in Mr. Frete's carefully guarded library at the age of twenty? and why were his lips so tightly compressed? He was sawing wood—working. An improvised bench had been erected in the light of the two windows that gave upon the back yard, and at it stood Miad, engaged in the most intricate of the vocations that old man Crabbe had taught him so thoroughly. At either side of him were bits of weird leathers, softly tanned: Snake skin, paper thin, glassy on one surface to the touch; the pale hide from the belly of a baby crocodile. Other parchments, still more gruesome, littered the working table and would have recalled to the *cognoscenti* rumors that Egyptian leather, most durable known to man, was unwillingly supplied by the Pharaohs' slaves.

Directly before him were the books he was to bind, and it was the nature of the thoughts aroused by these clandestine volumes that kept his lips set in a straight white line. He was thinking of Mr. Frete as of something viscid like a snail, slimy as the mucous reptiles whose hides he coveted for the books nearest to his heart. For such repellent bindings—and secrecy—this oily man was willing to pay the very top price of a very high market. From time to time Miad would remember that Cornelia, the sweetest contact of all his life with a single exception, had been an inmate of this house.

At such moments a lump would pop into his throat, his heart would sink down and down, and he would stop work and glare unseeingly out of the window.

Who was this sleek beast, Mr. Frete, and who was his needle-nosed sister? Whence had they come into Cornelia's life? What had they to do with her? Why had she never opened her lips in regard to them? The house in which he found himself in the due course of business answered in part that last question. Considered as a whole, it was extremely commonplace; beheld in the side light of the scrofulous library, all its shadows became sinister.

Now Miad could understand without words the instinct that had led Cornelia, gay, imaginative, hugry for the sunshine of happiness, to turn her mind as she turned her back upon its peculiar gloom whenever occasion offered. Mr. Frete—Cornelia! He could not bracket them in the same thought. It was like trying to imagine the white splash of leprosy against healthy young flesh. Thank God she was away; pray God she might never come back!

On the second day after Cornelia's return, unknown to Miad, just after she had helped Amantha Frete clear the table of the midday meal she went up to her room on the third floor and chanced to look out of the window across East Broadway. For an instant she thought she dreamed; then, with one hand to her breast and the other holding the lawn curtains slightly apart, with her eyes sparkling and her lips quirking at the corners in silent laughter, she watched Mr. Harold Grimble, Master of Arts, alumnus of Yale, sometime member of the glee club and the football squad, walk up and down the opposite sidewalk with comical indecision, look at his watch, stop to stare at the house on the corner of Market Street, walk up and down, look at his watch again, stop again, start to cross, return to the curb, and, finally, make a determined dash.

GREAT VAN SUTTART MYSTERY

By pressing her face against the glass Cornelia was able to witness the accosting of Mr. Frete by Mr. Grimble. Mr. Frete was already late in returning to his place of business and, besides, he was not accustomed to being addressed by total strangers. He answered the eager question over his shoulder sharply. A look of surprise and a deep flush swept over Mr. Grimble's face. He stood staring rather vapidly at the door from which Mr. Frete had issued, then turned and actually walked away! Vanish smile from Cornelia's eyes and lips. An astonished fatal pause. Quick! Open the window! Oh, treacherous catch! Run—run down the stairs. Faster. Faster! Throw open the front door, step out upon the stoop, glance down the crowded yet empty street. Alas! he is gone.

"What on earth are you doing, Cornelia?" said a voice at her back.

"Nothing, Miss Frete. The—the house seemed very close. I wished to go out."

"What! Without a hat?"

"It is true," said Cornelia with a pathetic droop of her lips which had so lately quirked to a mischievous smile. "I forgot my hat. I will fetch it."

When she came down a few minutes later she found Miss Frete ready to accompany her.

"Please do not bother, Miss Frete. I wish to go alone."

"Prosper would not like that, Cornelia. You must not forget that you are a grown young lady, so grown that he wishes you to call me Amantha and also to know and think of him by his given name."

"I could never do that," murmured Cornelia. "I might call you Amantha if you yourself wish it, but—not the other."

"Some day," said Miss Frete, eyeing her with a strained bradawl look which strove vainly to appear sentimental, "you will know all that you owe Prosper. In that day your heart will cry out his name from gratitude alone."

Cornelia's response would have been far dif-

ferent had this appeal occurred half an hour
earlier, but somehow, with the memory fresh
in mind of the blank look that had come over
Harold Grimble's eager face at hearing certain curt words from Mr. Frete's lips, she did
not experience any marked softening of the
heart toward Amantha or her self-sacrificing
brother. As she walked along she even felt
that her companion's presence was more than
superfluous. It dragged upon her, heavy as
ball and chain, for there was just one thing she
wished to do. She wished to go to Cobbled
Court. She wished to see Miad.

It is possible that her impulse to turn to
Cobbled Court and Miad in the hour of need
was due merely to the lasting grip of happy
associations, but it is also possible that the
motive was imbedded in the very foundations
of instinct. Miad was closer than lover; dearer
than friend. Why? She did not know. It
had always been so, from the very first day,
without words, without question and without
solution. Just as he had been wont to say of

herself, "She ain't my girl; she's just Cornelia," so was Miad just Miad to her thoughts and heart, and now she wanted to see him.

You who read know how supremely natural was the bond of sympathy that existed between them. Neither Cornelia nor Miad had ever paused to question it; and yet, of course, there was a reason for the bond—such a reason as, had they known it, would have transformed the entire universe to each of them. At that time Brooklyn was still Brooklyn, and New York only New York, but even so, the city proper numbered considerably more than a million souls. Out of this million odd living human beings only one could have scratched his wiry head and said, "Miad, me boy, tell me now, wasn't your mother's born name Mary Malone?" or turned and said, "Miss Cornelia, young lady, ain't nobody ever told you your mother's born name was Mary Malone?"

Totally unconscious of this one person— this lone needle in the haystack of humanity

—Cornelia knew only that she wished to see Miad and that Miss Frete's presence made that consummation impossible. She walked along at some speed, but aimlessly, saying nothing to her unwelcome companion, and with her eyes down. The eyes are the barometer of life's weather. When we are gay we look up; when we are depressed we look down. Nevertheless something made Cornelia look up in time to see a street sign that caused her to turn to the left almost without thinking and suddenly quicken her stride. If she could not see Miad she could do the next best thing: she could see his father! When they reached the entrance to the Eden Musée she paused, stared at the flaming billboards, and presently insisted on entering.

Miss Frete demurred, but only for a moment. When a young lady of eighteeen has been traveling with head down and then suddenly lifts it, there is just one thing to do— follow on and keep your eyes open. Once within the portals of the wax-works empor-

ium, Cornelia constrained herself to many cal-
culated pauses. She forced herself to take an
interest in the effigy of the martyred Garfield
and to come to a full stop before President
Arthur—in life, dignified, sartorially correct;
in wax, a caricature, terrible to behold. She
identified the fake policeman and strove without success to recognize the live one whom she
had kicked on the shin on that breathless day
when she and Miad, side by side, had redis-
covered the silent companion of many a happy
hour spent in the cellar beneath Crabbe's won-
drous shop.

Finally she sidled into the corner of that
bygone revelation and raised her eyes slowly to
the placid, the beloved face of John Blake,
preserved.

There may be encounters more poignant to
memory than that of Cornelia face to face with
Miad's father—the father in whom she had
been granted a half share long after he was
dead—but none more lovely in their pathos.
To be beautiful and alone is a terrible fate.

[223]

GREAT VAN SUTTART MYSTERY

Even the full heart of freckled youth demands sympathy, admiration and comfort by right, and finds it in most unexpected places. Miad, starved of so many of the bounties due to childhood, had known content in the meager companionship of his embalmed father, and here was Cornelia come to the same still source for consolation.

Something of the untutored uprightness, something of the rough-hewn yet indescribably gentle strength of John Blake in life, must have endured through the cunning of old Crabbe's art. Else why should this exquisite bud on the branch of womanhood have thrilled and swayed before the ineffable peace in the dead man's face, and drunk deep of the soft dew of solace?

Wake up, Cornelia! Look behind you! Look at Miss Amantha Frete! See a shock pass in through her tiny eyes and out through her toes, leaving her rigid, all but her sharp proboscis. The tip of her nose quivers, squirms and twists in minute circles as if striving des-

perately to bore into the mystery before her.
Needle-pointed questions writhe off it in
staccato vibrations.

Miss Frete is thinking at a speed her brain
has never before attained. John Blake! Is it
indeed John Blake, the wartime porter of
Hendricks, Jacob Hendricks, Van Suttart and
Partners—that ancient, half-forgotten firm,
so different from the Van Suttart & Co. of
today! The John Blake who knew the elder
Van Suttart? Who was said to have reeled
and fainted with joy at the return of William
Van Suttart from the dead? Who undoubtedly
knew Mary Malone Van Suttart, Cornelia's
mother? John Blake, who, should he open
those lifelike lips and speak, could——

Then, even more breathlessly, she thought:
Cornelia! Why, what—what did Cornelia
know of *him?* Of the porter—John Blake?

At this instant Cornelia passed on quietly to
a ghastly murder reconstruction which had
been in former times a favorite of hers and
Miad's. Now it gave her no thrill save one of

laughing horror at its crudity. She could smile at it only because the sight of John Blake had by some mysterious alchemy lifted up her heart. When Miss Frete, having regained a semblance of equanimity, plucked at her sleeve and suggested that it was time to go, she was ready.

CHAPTER XIII

IN THE CLAWS OF THE DRAGON

THAT evening, after Cornelia had gone up to bed, she gradually became conscious of a strange sound, and then wondered why it was strange. Fresh from the chattering clatter of Barmingdale, she had failed immediately to readjust herself to the lifelong peculiarities of the gloomy house in East Broadway. The sound was strange because never before had she heard within those walls the murmuring of voices. The inarticulate communion of years between the Fretes, male and female, had become vocal! So remote was the whispering, so accustomed was she to sleep the moment her glossy head touched the pillow, that she failed to detect a tone of faint, questioning alarm in the voices.

[227]

GREAT VAN SUTTART MYSTERY

On the following day Mr. Frete was not himself. He came down meticulously dressed, but did not go to business. Instead he went for the first time in his life to the Eden Musée, and on the way thought of the absurdly young man who had asked if Miss Cornelia Van Suttart was at home and had looked so markedly crestfallen when informed that she had gone to Europe for the summer. Further proof that Prosper was not himself can be found in the fact that when he returned to the house he did not think to enter the library, where Miad was working doggedly, determined to finish on that very day a distasteful job.

Miad had come in simultaneously with the iceman through the areaway and gone up a narrow spiral stairway into the room from which even Miss Amantha Frete was excluded except for the forenoon of the first Monday in every quarter, when after locking certain of the inclosed bookcases, Mr. Frete permitted her to dust and clean. It thus transpired that while Miad munched a sandwich in the library the Fretes and Cornelia partook of a silent meal in the dining room. Nor did Mr. Frete leave immediately thereafter. Instead, when the table was cleared and Cornelia, as was her custom, started to go to her room, he stopped her, took her by the hand and led her into the front parlor. Miss Frete abandoned her household duties rather ostentatiously and went upstairs.

"Cornelia," said Mr. Frete, still holding her hand, "the time has come when you and I must arrive at an understanding."

"An understanding, Mr. Frete?" asked Cornelia, instinctively sparring for time.

"Yes, my dear," continued Mr. Frete in his fullest voice. "I asked you through Amantha to call me Prosper. I now beg it of you myself. All your life I have watched over you and slaved for you. So far my only reward has been to see you grow from an abandoned babe into a resplendent woman. I never talked to you as a child. Do you know why? Because deep within me I have known always that the day of love would come and that I would need all the words of a lifetime to tell you of it."

"Oh, Mr. Frete!" cried Cornelia, striving to withdraw her hand. "Please, Mr. Frete. Please!"

"Don't," murmured Mr. Frete softly, even while he retained a firm hold. "Don't be frightened. Don't draw away from me. Listen, my dear Cornelia. Once within my arms I will carry you to worlds of which you have never dreamed. Do not struggle. Let me hold you close. Let me whisper to you of the mysteries and the wonders of all-embracing love."

"Oh, Mr. Frete! Please! Please let me go!"

"No; no! I cannot let you go," cried Mr. Frete, in dead earnest. "Not until I have told you. Not until you have promised to be my own wife."

Quite suddenly Cornelia yielded to his importunity. Feeling her tense body relax, he released his hold in order to take her in his arms, but in the instant before he could do so she quickly drew up both hands, placed them against his chest and pushed him away with all her strength. Her wide eyes were no longer pleading nor frightened; they blazed.

"Go away!" she cried. "Don't you dare to touch me again. I do not love you. I cannot love you. You are an old man."

The transformation that swept over Mr. Frete was so instantaneous as to be amazing. In the twinkling of an eye he had balanced all the chances for persuasion against the permanence of Cornelia's determination, and found them wanting. The foresight that had never yet failed him told him that never as long as she lived would she give herself to him willingly. The light in his eyes changed to a threatening gleam. His sleek head shot forward and his hands came up very slowly from his sides.

"Call out," he whispered hoarsely, "and no one will hear. Scream, and no one will come. Before you leave this room, you ungrateful little waif, you will go on your knees and beg me to marry you."

He did not rush at her; he came slowly, and as he moved Cornelia knew fear. Her eyes opened wider and wider. A lump surged into her throat. The blood pounded deafeningly in her ears and temples. She stepped backward and backward until she came against the wall. She extended her arms, pressed her open palms flat against the wall, raised her white face, closed her eyes.

"Miad," she murmured, half sobbing. "Oh, Miad!" Then suddenly she screamed it out loud with all the strength of her lungs. "Miad!"

As she screamed she felt Mr. Frete's hot breath upon her cheek and his hands clutching at her throat, tearing shamefully as though they would rip the clothing from her body. She struck furiously but ineffectually with her closed fists at his lowered head.

Beyond the dining room the great doors of the library slid apart and Miad stepped out.

IN THE CLAWS OF THE DRAGON

For an instant he stood blinking, glancing to right and left as if he had been abruptly awakened from deep sleep; then his startled eyes awoke, comprehended, narrowed. His short body, already compact, seemed to draw together tighter and tighter. It was as though some alien force were molding him into a round bullet and drawing him back and back in the sling of a catapult.

Snap the catch. Loose the trigger. Let the bullet fly. Shades of Mr. Levis and the fight of long ago in Cobbled Court, see the ball of fury hurtle across the floor! Look out, Mr. Frete! Look out!

From ten feet away Miad shot into the air, landing with the heel of his heavy boot on Mr. Frete's left leg, just below the knee. He had meant to break the leg and failed only because its muscles were so taut that it withstood the terrific strain. Even so, Mr. Frete reeled and fell under the excruciating blow, perforce releasing Cornelia at the same time. She opened her eyes and stared incredulously.

Miad? Why, it couldn't be Miad. Oh, miracle! Oh, potent prayer! Oh, faith! It was. It was Miad. Miad pouncing on the prone Mr. Frete, groping with stubby iron hands for Mr. Frete's throat, finding it, squeezing it, and changing his mind presently as Mr. Frete's protruding tongue began to blacken. Miad getting his fingers into Mr. Frete's long, sleek hair, gripping it and then beginning to pound Mr. Frete's head rhythmically on the floor.

From Mr. Frete's released throat a horrible, raucous sound, scarcely distinguishable, began to issue at regular spaced intervals:

"Help! Help! Help!"

Miad looked up from his task. "Run, Corny. You know where. Run there and wait. Do what I say, Corny."

Cornelia gathered her senses and started obediently for the door. Too late. Miss Frete, having entered the room, was just turning the key in the lock. Cornelia met her eyes and trembled. Never in her life had she seen such a look. What doors were locked? How get out? Which way? Which way was surest? She rushed into the dining room and her eyes fell on the cavernous dumb-waiter. Without a pause to think of the possible consequences she climbed into it, gave the rope a pull and let the heavy box crash to the basement floor. Presently came her voice.

"All right, Miad. Do you hear? All right."

Had it not been for Amantha Frete it is probable that in the end Miad Blake would have cracked Mr. Frete's skull and been forced, sooner or later, to stand trial for murder. In a manner of speaking it was fortunate for him that Miss Frete before entering the room had found time to snatch a long hatpin of a fashion now mercifully obsolete from the hall table. Thus armed she slithered across the parlor and with more venom than anatomical science drove her murderous weapon deep into Miad's back. He flinched from the sharp pain, but did not cry out. Instead, instantly aware of his peril, he let go his hold on

Mr. Frete's hair, threw himself flat and rolled.

Miss Frete pursued him, holding the hatpin parallel with her scarcely less pointed nose, whose tip quivered and gyrated as if it were a seismograph needle indicating a terrific internal convulsion. Miad whirled on his back preparatory to kicking her with both feet, but thought better of it. Scorning to manhandle a woman, he reached out, caught her skirts and gave them such a violent pull as no waistband could withstand.

Oh, Barmingdale three-leafed screen, impenetrable guardian of maiden blushes where art thou now? Miss Frete dropped the hatpin, clutched at her falling petticoats and screamed. Miad leaped to his feet, jumped over the body of the groaning Mr. Frete, dashed into the library, down the spiral stairs and out through the area door, which Cornelia in her haste had left wide open.

At this point in the narrative of Miad Blake and Cornelia Van Suttart, steps in history, ready as usual to repeat itself, only with a difference. Go back to the fall of 1870. Do you remember how John Blake, staggered by the discovery that the woman he thought to be his wife was another's, hovered tenderly, day after day, outside the room where Mary Malone was going through the torment of abandoning her firstborn for his good and her own honor before God?

John Blake had been at his greatest in that rôle of sacrificial victim. Now behold Miad, John's son and Mary Malone's son, doing a like thing outside the same room, except that it was for Cornelia Van Suttart—and with a difference. The commotion that was shaking Cornelia's breast during these days could not be called a torment by any stretch of the word.

Name it adventure, or awakening, or romance, or just love. Call it any old thing as long as you realize how she looked and felt and moved within the hidden room in Cobbled Court where Miad Blake was born. Outside, Mr. Frete and certain paid agents, watching the front entrance to the house, guarding both ends of Hague Street, the alley under the northern eaves of Brooklyn Bridge and the great gate and greater arch which looked toward Cliff Street. Within, Cornelia, wondering by day how long her pulses could beat so fast without bursting, and at night, piloted by Miad, creeping stealthily down the stairs, through the shop, through the cellar, through the long passage to a vaultlike chamber beneath Hague Street, where sat beside a scarred workbench, lighted by a single candle, Old Man Crabbe—and Mr. Harold Grimble, summoned by Miad at Cornelia's instance.

What did they talk about, these four most diverse persons in the history of the somnolent city of New York? Well, for the most part they speculated aloud on the strange procedure of Mr. Frete, which indicated sinister strength and at the same time proclaimed some suspected but as yet undiscovered weakness. Since he seemed to know that Cornelia was within, why didn't he call the police and drag her out?

IN THE CLAWS OF THE DRAGON

Harold was all for calling in his father, stepping out in the open and fighting the strength, whatever it proved to be; but the minds of Mr. Crabbe and of Miad congenitally lingered on the note of weakness. If there was some reason why Mr. Frete dared not accuse them of abduction and bring in the law to aid him in resuming guardianship over the person of Cornelia Van Suttart, spinster, there were a dozen reasons why old man Crabbe and his youthful partner preferred to let him have his way and, in the end, beat him at his own game. In other words, they felt more at ease with things illicit than licit and the mere mention of Mr. Grimble in his capacity of lawyer made them squirm.

Naturally they got tired of talking about Mr. Frete and what he could or would do in the course of time. At such moments Mr. Crabbe, who was growing doddering old, would fall into reminiscence of pre-war days and describe the workings of the Underground Route so graphically that the damp dark chamber and its darker exits would teem with white eyes, shining from black, negro faces; and Cornelia would draw closer still to Harold, even letting him hold her hand. Sometimes these two murmured *sotto voce* to each other, but what they said is nobody's business. Miad, for the most part, was purposefully silent. When at last he decided to speak he talked for half an hour without stopping, and every word that fell from his lips was strictly to the point.

"It's this way," he concluded. "The way I see it is that Mr. Frete wants to marry Cornelia, see? Whatever Mr. Frete wants is what we don't want, see? Now we don't know what will make her marry him, but we do know just one thing that will surely make it so he can't, see? Harold, you got to marry Cornelia and do it quick."

Harold's eyes lighted for an instant, and then he turned a deep red.

"Miad," he said, holding tightly to Cornelia's hand, "there isn't anything on earth I want to do except marry Cornelia. But listen,

Miad; listen, Mr. Crabbe. What my father pays me at present wouldn't keep two sparrows alive. He even has to feed me."

"That's all right," replied Miad. "Cornelia ain't a pauper, Harold. She's had three thousand dollars in the bank at compound interest ever since she helped get the reward for the Luxendorf pearls. If you're too all-fired proud to borrow from her and start on that —why, I guess me or Mr. Crabbe will have to marry her. What do you say, Cornelia?"

Cornelia gave him a deep and tender glance. "I think," she said gently, "perhaps I'll marry Harold, if you don't mind, Miad."

"Naw, I don't mind," said Miad—and he meant it.

Two days later at half past eleven a scout rushed off to find Mr. Frete and inform him that a smart carriage and pair had entered and come to an inexplicable stop in the narrow gullet of Hague Street. Ten minutes later Mr. Frete was accosting the coachman and getting not even a glance for his pains. Two minutes later he dashed boldly into Crabbe's shop, where he came face to face with the old man himself.

"Listen to me!" he cried. "What funny business are you and that dirty little swipe of a partner of yours up to? I've gone easy with you so far for reasons of my own, but if you think you can abduct an innocent young girl and get away without the law putting you where you belong for the rest of your natural life, guess again, Mr. Crabbe. Guess again!"

Mr. Crabbe had heard that sort of language at least once before. He laid down the tool with which he was working, pushed his glasses high on his forehead and eyed the irate Mr. Frete for a calm long moment. When he spoke his voice and words were as smooth as butter.

"I'm sorry, Mr. Frete; indeed I am. I don't know what will become of me and my business on account of that Miad Blake. You wait here, Mr. Frete, and I'll see what I can do. Indeed I will, Mr. Frete."

IN THE CLAWS OF THE DRAGON

The old man went to the back of the shop, descended the stairs into the cellar, made sure that Mr. Frete was not following, dodged into the long underground passage and emerged in the front room, wooden shutters closed, of the middle one of the five houses on the south side of Hague Street. He was just in time. In that very room, at high noon on the twenty-ninth day of July, 1890, as is witnessed by the signatures of old man Crabbe, of Mike the stable hand, and of Miad Blake, who lied about his age, the marriage of Cornelia Van Suttart and Harold Grimble was lawfully solemnized.

The narrow door of the house in Hague Street opened outward, striking against the wheels of the waiting carriage and making the horses plunge. The scout dashed into Cobbled Court in search of Mr. Frete. Down the three steep steps of the house in Hague Street came Harold Grimble, his hatless bride upon his arm. Around the corner from Cobbled Court rushed Mr. Frete.

Feeling the weight of passengers on the

carriage step, the horses champed their bits and pawed the cobblestones. The coachman gave them their heads. As they dashed away toward Pearl, Mr. Crabbe, in spectacles and leather apron, stepped into the center of Hague Street, directly in the path of the oncoming Mr. Frete.

"Say, where do you think you're going?" asked the old man with a toothless leer. "Won't the place wait for you?"

"Going!" muttered Mr. Frete venomously, coming to a sudden stop. "I'll show you where I'm going, you white-headed jailbird! I'm going to have the law on you! That's where I'm going!"

"I wonder," said Mr. Crabbe coolly, pinching his underlip and boring with gimlet eyes into his erstwhile patron. "I wonder a lot; I do indeed, Mr. Frete, and I'll tell you why. I grant you a skunk can defend himself, but— can he go to law?"

CHAPTER XIV

MIAD GETS THE SCENT OF MYSTERY

THE saddest conflicts in life are the battles of misunderstanding which happen only to frank and basically lovable people. The minds of all such persons have the selfsame bolting quality that distinguishes a runaway horse. All masters of indirection, all shrewd people, all involuted thinkers such as old man Crabbe and Miad Blake, as well as all human weasels such as Mr. Levis, automatically escape the disasters attendant upon taking the bit in one's mental mouth. Lawyer Grimble and his son Harold, on the other hand, were exceptionally frank individuals.

If only Harold had said to the elder Grimble, "Father, do you remember when I was a

kid there was some cock-and-bull story about
the disappearance of the entire Van Suttart
family? How they cleared out with all their
own money and left a baby girl behind? Well,
she's grown up into one of the most extraordinary creatures you ever saw. Beautiful,
well-bred. Gee! I wish you could talk to her.
I saw her at Barmingdale."

With that opening gambit Harold would
have immediately drawn from his father a two-
hour reminiscent summary of the great Van
Suttart mystery. He would not only have put
his father's mind in harness but would have
held both reins and the whiphand. He could
have driven him gently but at a rapid pace up
to the point where the elder Grimble's face
would have glowed with pride at the news of
his son's marriage. He could have gained
from the very start a stalwart ally. Did he do
these things?

Well, put yourself in his place. Consider
that he had just turned twenty-two and remember, if you can, how twenty-two could love

Cornelia Van Suttart at eighteen. Recollect the matter-of-fact manner in which Miad had declared that someone had to marry Cornelia in a hurry; if not Harold, then himself or old man Crabbe. Lose her? Never. Money or no money, he had to marry her. He did. They drove away from the house in Hague Street. With all the cash in his pockets and some more that Miad had thrust into his hand, Cornelia bought herself a hat and certain other things, less conventional but more necessary. Then they drove around some more and finally returned for their honeymoon to Cobbled Court and the room where Miad Blake was born.

In that breathless journey there had been no moment in which to think of father and mother or what he should say or do, but when Cornelia fell asleep it was different. Cobbled Court at night was very quiet. A summer moon slanted through the open window of the second-story front and glorified with its reflected radiance all the meager furnishings of the abode that had been the scene of such extraordinary happenings in lives of apparent inconsequence.

Here John Blake, porter, had given refuge to Mary Malone Van Suttart in the day of her greatest need. Here he had married, lived with her and loved her. Here she had met the terrific blow of the news that her husband, William Van Suttart, had returned from the war and the dead. Here she had known utter agony and triumphed, surrendering her firstborn, at the behest of an inexorable fate. Here John Blake had understood and continued unshaken in his love to the day of his death. Here the baby, Miad, orphaned, had become the son of the city of New York and set out at a tender age to take life as it came, by assault.

Is it stretching the point to believe that nobility of action and conduct can infect a locality for good? There are rooms that are irreparably stained by the people who have lived in them, and why not the opposite? However that may be, Harold Grimble felt something new spring up within him as he

looked at the young girl who had become forever an integral part of himself. Propped upon his elbow, he saw that her hair was a smoky
cloud, black as ink upon the white pillow, a
dark nest that lifted her lovely face to his
gaze. The normal pallor of her cheeks held a
faint pink glow, deep down, under the petal
surface of the skin. Her fallen lashes were
startlingly vivid, fantastical, like black cres-
cent moons against a clear sky. But her
parted lips were real, human, incomparably
sweet. To look at them made his heart swell
to the verge of bursting.

What could not a man do for such a girl?
Burn the candle. Pay the piper. Face the
music. Do you begin to get the mood that
possessed Harold when in the morning he first
talked things over with Miad and then in-
trusted Cornelia to Miad's guardianship while
he walked, head up and shoulders squared,
straight to his father's office and in? Do you
wonder that he scarcely heard the elder Grimble's tight-lipped request for an explanation

of a night-long absence that had banished sleep from an entire household and driven Harold's invalid mother to distraction?

"Father, I'm married."

"What!"

"I'm married to the—"

"Stop! Wait a minute! One thing at a time. You are twenty-two years old, a few weeks out of college, and you were getting fifty dollars a month. You have read law for ten days, but aside from that you probably know what constitutes a marriage. Now, can you say again that you are married?"

Harold, tossing back his head and looking his father straight in the eye: "Yes, sir. But—"

"That's enough," interrupted Mr. Grimble, leaning forward. "Get out of here! Get out, and don't come back! I'd rather have a madman with a stick of dynamite in each pocket around the office than you. By golly, if it wasn't too late to do any good I believe I could thrash you!"

MIAD GETS THE SCENT OF MYSTERY

Harold, gulping shamefully: "You try it! You just try it! Listen. She's—"

Mr. Grimble, pounding his desk with a violence that drowned his son's words and turning more purple at each repetition: "Get out! Get out! Get out!"

That is what comes of frankness without circumspection. Harold walked out of his father's office to look for a job and to face several years of the hardest kind of sledding. He and Cornelia moved to a very small house in Waverly Place. The first baby came on the seventeenth of August, 1891, an extraordinarily hot day, and was named Harold Van Suttart Grimble; the second baby came just a year and a month later and was called Cornelia Van Suttart Grimble. The first of these advents saw the finish of Cornelia's four-thousand-dollar bank account, and the second forced the acceptance, under protest, of the last of Miad's surplus cash. Things looked blacker and blacker for Harold, for Cornelia and their youngsters, and—by indirection—for

Miad, Mr. Crabbe and anyone who by any stretch of circumstance might possibly bring aid to the hard-pressed couple.

Old man Crabbe dated the blight that had fallen on his establishment in Cobbled Court from the day on which Miad Blake, at the age of eleven, had shown a congenital honest streak. It may be argued that Miad had not been consciously honest when he deprived Mr. Levis of the profits accruing to the skillful smuggling of three magnificent stolen pearls, but Mr. Crabbe was a wizard at perceiving fundamentals. Whether Miad knew or did not know himself to be honest was neither here nor there; what mattered was that his act had betrayed an inclination to travel in a straight line and damn the consequences. That he had hated Mr. Levis and wished no truck with him at any price was merely a corollary.

Miad dated hard work from the same occasion; but not real, dyed in the wool trouble. Mr. Levis had been the source of much annoyance and had finally succeeded in hound-ing the embalmed body of John Blake from his long home in the cellar under Crabbe's shop to a short sojourn in Dutchy Eckstrom's place and from there to a precarious haven in the Eden Musée; but so far he had failed in his main purpose, which was to railroad Miad Blake's father into the grave. He had driven him into dignified seclusion but not into the ground, where John Blake would spoil.

By the way and as a matter of idle curiosity, where are the once-famous waxworks of the Eden Musée? Where are the personages, the royalty, the murderers and murdered that once graced those halls of notoriety? Where are all those pink-cheeked and goggle-eyed atrocities that entertained and improved—save the mark!—the young of a bygone generation?

For most of Miad's and Cornelia's old familiar friends among that galaxy let ragman and ashcan answer, but not for John Blake, who resides, unburied to this day, in a chaste, templelike structure in Greenwood Cemetery.

He is arranged in a vault which bears, be-

sides his own, the family name of Crabbe.
There is a bronze door, and a small high
window which sheds on John Blake's peaceful
countenance just such a soft light as used
to illumine it back in the days of Miad's
childhood and of the cellar under Mr. Crabbe's
shop. But wait. Halt. We have skidded
thirty years.

Miad Blake dated all real trouble from the
summer of 1890, when he engineered the marriage of Cornelia Van Suttart and Harold
Grimble by the underground route, yet, para-
doxically, over the head of Mr. Prosper Frete.
Considered in the light of events that came to
pass subsequently, the enmity of Mr. Levis,
long quiescent, dwindled almost to the vanishing point. As an enemy Mr. Levis, when
compared to Mr. Frete, was less than a spar-
rowhawk; he was a mere barnyard catbird.
For Mr. Frete combined in himself the attributes of a baldheaded eagle and the propensities of a mole. He worked from high above
and from deep below; his animosity recognized

no limits and was as merciless as the Infinite
and almost as omnipresent.

What bothered Miad most was that this
active hatred was not directed at him alone, but
against Cornelia, against old man Crabbe,
against Harold Grimble and even against Mr.
Grimble, although the lawyer had never weak-
ened for a moment in his determination to
have nothing to do with a scatterbrained
son, and remained in pig-headed ignorance of
whom that son had rashly married. A long
time, you will say, for father and son to hold a
grudge. Well, think it out. A successful dis-
inherited son bobs up under his father's nose
on the first high wave; an unsuccessful one, if
he has any guts, keeps out of his father's way.

Miad was acquainted with grudges and had
observed at close quarters a large variety of
feuds, but the unflagging enmity of Mr. Frete
was something different, something beyond his
ken. It puzzled him, and from his infancy
to be puzzled short of a solution was nothing
less than torment. There were certain per-

sons who had it in for you and gave you a dig whenever they got the chance. That was all right. In the long run they either forgot their grouch or you learned never to give them a chance. But here was a man who did not know when to quit, a sinister influence that reached over, under and around an entire group of people with a bulldog pertinacity that was surely choking the life out of them. Why? In his perplexity Miad decided to tap the source of all knowledge; he went to Mr. Crabbe.

"Fine," said the old man sarcastically. "Oh, fine! Get yourself all messed up through being too gol-durned honest, and then come to an old crook to learn you how it happened. You couldn't let me and Mr. Levis get rich overnight. Oh, no. You couldn't let this here Mr. Frete marry a long-legged girl you didn't want yourself, and keep on sending us orders. Oh, no. You couldn't make that Grimble boy lie sensible to his father about what he been and done, and keep Cornelia dark for a while.

Oh, no. You can't even let them two young fools and their babies starve to death and tend to your own business. Oh, no."

"Say," interrupted Miad, "what's the matter with you? Didn't you help them get married? Wasn't it you swore that Cornelia was of age? Didn't you take your Bible oath you was in Van Suttart's office the day she was born, and heard about it? Didn't Harold marry her just so you and me wouldn't have to? Weren't you going to fall into Frete's trap of another mortgage on this here place only yesterday so you could give the money to her? You make me sick. You're getting too old to think."

"Old!" grunted Mr. Crabbe, leaning forward in the high chair he had contrived for the harboring of his declining strength. It was an extraordinary contraption with broad hickory arms and a strong rung in which he could catch his heels. Perched in it, with glasses pushed high into his snow-white hair, he looked like a gray gnome, all cavernous

eyes and a whisp of mist for a body. "Old?
Ha! Well, there is them as might call me old
in a manner of speaking, and then again, there
ain't; 'cause they're all dead, see? Why, son,
I been old since before you was born right upstairs, over our heads. Yes, sir. John Blake,
him we preserved as mortal sweet as a jar of
spiced peaches, him was your father."

Suddenly Miad forgot his impatience. He
hitched himself to a seat on the ancient workbench where he had sat through various epoch-
making occasions of his life since before the
age of three.

"Yes, Crabbe," he said with childlike fer-
vency. "I remember him; but what about my
mother?"

"Your mother, now," said the old man,
puckering his withered lips. "Oh, she was just
one o' them wimmen."

"Yes," persisted Miad, his eyes gleaming
belligerently, "of course she was just a woman.
But what was she like, Crabbe? What did she
look like? You tell me."

The old man tried honestly to remember. "Well," he said at last, "she was kind of dark-favored. Fine eyes, she had, gentle ways and a soft voice. When I first seen her she was the spit o' that long-legged girl, only older than her is now."

"Do you mean Cornelia?" asked Miad.

The old man nodded. "Your father, John Blake that was, must have worked for Corny's father or grandfather; I dunno which," he continued, apparently letting his thoughts wander at random along the channel of least resistance. "Porter he was; porter around to Hendricks', Jacob Hendricks, Van Suttart and Partners as was. Then he got sick. Folks said he was sick; but I ain't never seen nobody could twirl a case lighter than what he could when he was supposed to be ailing. No, sir. And after that the whole Van Suttart family disappeared. Yes, sir. Lock, stock and barrel. All on 'em except this here baby."

"Cornelia?" demanded Miad, slipping off the edge of the bench and standing poised, while his mind raced this way and that like a hound on a first true scent.

"Well, I dunno," said the old man indifferently. "It's nothing but guessing, come to think on it. Seeing of her name all writ out when I was fool enough to swear to that preacher I knowed her when she was born made me think she must of been kin to old Skinflint Van Suttart. Dead or alive, I hope I done him a bad turn."

There ensued a long silence, during which Miad never moved. Finally he broke it.

"Crabbe," he asked, "don't you think it's kind of funny the way Mr. Frete has kept after all on us so long? There ain't nothing mean and nasty that has happened to us since that pig-eyed Levis let up but what I could run it back to the door of Mr. Prosper Frete. Why don't he get tired and quit? It ain't only me and you. He's bought seven jobs away from Harold. Never mind how I found out; I did, all right. And now here's this case in the papers where it looks like he's got Harold's old man tied up in three kinds of knots, and Mr. Grimble never even speaking to Harold since the day after he was married. Think a minute. Ain't it funny?"

"Funny!" scoffed the old man. "It's so funny I'm 'mazed you and me don't laugh ourselves to death instead of starving. Funny? Bah! What I say is this: With all the world to choose from, why in blazes did you have to pick on Levis and the Board of Health and the judge and this here Mr. Prosper Frete to stamp on their foot for? Why couldn't you look around for something soft and easy about your own size to let your honesty chew on? I make you sick, do I? Well, you make me sick. Gol durn it, I'm hungry and I can't even give you work to get even with you."

"I guess perhaps you're right about honesty, Crabbe," said Miad, turning to the bench, picking up a tool and twirling it listlessly. "I guess perhaps it don't pay to be honest and stupid. From now on I quit."

"What you mean, Miad?" asked the old

man, suddenly dropping the carping tone out of his voice. "You going to do something crooked? You going to quit being honest, Miad?"

"No," said Miad, jabbing the tool into the bench. "I mean I'm going to quit being stupid. I'm going to make money or bust, and then I'm going to fill you so full of food you'll wish you was all belly, like a snake."

CHAPTER XV

BEYOND REACH OF THE LAW

DURING the next few months Miad kept his word to a surprising degree. He did it by thinking things out. At the moment Mr. Frete had the best of him. He would continue to have the best of him as long as he kept him bankrupt of cash, for there is nothing so helpless as a pauper. A pauper can't fight in any sense of the word. To climb up to the active plane of a worm a pauper has to die, when he attains to the faculty of boring a hole in some potter's field and hiding away. Mr. Frete's power was the power of unlimited cash behind a web of business associations it had taken a century to weave. Naturally that web had its limits. How far did it extend?

Miad hated even the appearance of running

away, but he made up his mind to swallow the bitter pill. The city had grown so tremendously during the score of years since he had become its son by force of circumstances that without leaving the vicinity of its crowded paths he could still move far from Mr. Frete's habitual orbit. After many wanderings he found what he wanted at the foot of West Fiftieth Street. On the northwest corner was a large warehouse, transformed later into trucking stables, and now a garage. On the river front a little stone-walled bay welcomed coal, lumber and brick scows. On the southwest corner was a large lot surrounded by a high board fence. Behind that fence were three shed-like structures and a shack. After the careful building of a few friendships and a little shrewd dickering Miad set up an office in the shack and a workshop in the nearest shed.

The false front to this subsidiary establishment was Harold Grimble. None of Crabbe's ancient patrons knew Harold by sight or had ever heard of him, but they soon came to the realization that here expert assistance of a great variety could be bought for ready money. Harold sneaked into the office by devious ways as early as he could make it and stayed there sometimes far into the night. He received all commissions, promised delivery according to a comprehensive schedule elaborated by Miad and took in the cash in due course.

Just here we collide with the question, What constitutes an honest man? Was Crabbe right in his contention that some people are born with honesty in them just as others are born with red hair? If so, can a man cheat the customs, perpetrate frauds on the public, deal in illicit wares, and still remain honest? Crabbe's philosophy says he can. It says more. It contends that all of us are honest to some of the people we meet and dishonest to others, in exact proportion as we are born with honesty in our veins. A thief who plays the game as he sees it without swerving off his individual straight road is an honest man within Mr. Crabbe's definition. Absurd, of course; non-sustainable, but peculiarly human when you think it out.

So we have Miad looking upon the contravention of certain laws as an honorable and highly skillful profession. Had a man called him a crook his eyes would have snapped wide open, and he would have gone promptly into action. In the case of a lady he would have reserved his fists and cried, "Why, I never stole nothing in my life nor done anyone a dirty trick that wasn't coming to them!" Crabbe's philosophy says these are the words of honesty.

However that may be, Miad connived with bargemen having contact with deep-sea vessels or the Canadian border, and also with young medical students and internes in need of cash. In the face of an oppressive law he supplied inquiring or gruesome minds and fat pocketbooks with human skulls and occasionally with an entire skeleton. Also for a price he made many a sound man look like a pitiful cripple during working hours only. In addition to all these things he reached out for legitimate commissions in taxidermy, bookbinding and special research, carefully evading the dropping of any clew that might draw Mr. Frete's attention to the new venture. Whenever possible he took such jobs to old man Crabbe when he returned at night to Cobbled Court. By limiting himself to forty-three cents a day for food, he not only kept the larders of his ancient partner and Cornelia supplied but gradually accumulated a fighting fund of twelve hundred dollars. When he reached that mark he was ready. He sought out Lawyer Grimble.

Is it strange that Miad should have known a lot better how to get at and talk to Mr. Grimble than did Mr. Grimble's own son? Not at all. Turn to the book of life and you will find that it was ever thus. In spite of his outlandish garments he annihiliated the office boy with a single look and triumphed almost as summarily over Mr. Grimble's secretary by calling her Clara, which happened to be her name. As once long ago, before anyone in the office knew quite how it happened, Miad Blake was standing, with feet slightly straddled, face to face with Harold's father.

"Remember me, Mr. Grimble?"

"No. Who said you could come in here? Wait a minute. Yes; sure I remember you. Miad Blake, single-handed, versus the Board of Health. Why, you haven't changed a bit. You haven't even grown. Are they trying again to bury your father?"

"No, sir," said Miad unsmilingly. "John Blake is all right up to the present. I didn't come to talk about him. I come because of something I seen in the papers and because of something else I suspicion that will make you sit up nights to keep your head from thinking itself clean off your neck."

"Really?" said Mr. Grimble, smiling broadly for the first time in many harassed weeks. "Sit down, Miad. I'll give you fifteen minutes. I have a feeling it will do me good."

"Do you good?" repeated Miad, his eyes bugging out belligerently. "Fifteen minutes? Why, at the end of fifteen minutes you'll be wishing I was your partner for life. Just for a starter, where was your nurse when you let one of Mr. Prosper Frete's straw men carry you for forty thousand dollars' worth of stock you couldn't pay for?"

Mr. Grimble leaped to his feet and turned red.

"What do you mean?" he snapped. "Where did you get that? Not from the papers?"

"Never mind where I got it," replied Miad, calmly retaining the seat he had taken. "And don't you get huffy with me, Mr. Grimble, until you've heard what I come to tell you. After that, you can't get huffy if you try. You sit down yourself and I'll tell you what happened while you take a rest."

"All right," said Mr. Grimble, scowling as he sat down. "Go ahead."

"It was this way," complied Miad. "Somebody come to you and got chummy and doped out a proposition that looked like raspberries in winter. They liked you so much they offered to give you a free ride on one of them sunk bear traps called a gentleman's agreement. Why did you fall? I'll tell you that too. Because you couldn't figure out any reason for them wanting to do you dirt. Ever since you found out it was Mr. Frete had his two thumbs in the soft part of your neck, things has been darker than ever. You can't see what the hell for Mr. Frete is picking on you. Right this minute you're going nutty trying to figure out why. Is that right?"

During Miad's masterly summary Mr. Grimble's attitude had entirely changed. He tapped the blotter before him absently with a paper cutter and stared vacantly at nothing in the room.

"Can you tell me why?" he asked.

"Perhaps I can and perhaps I can't," answered Miad, "but anyway I won't, because I got something importanter than that. I don't like this here Prosper Frete no more than what you do. What I want to do is to fix it so you can send him to the pen for twenty years."

BEYOND REACH OF THE LAW

"What?" cried Mr. Grimble, and threw back his head and laughed mirthlessly but long.

There is a saying that it takes two to make a quarrel, and the same is often true of a laugh. At the end of ten seconds Mr. Grimble, chancing to look at Miad's expressionless face, suddenly felt like a fool. He changed his laugh into a nervous cough.

"That's better," said Miad. "Now you listen to me, Mr. Grimble. About twenty-two years ago old Van Suttart, him as they called Skinflint, his son and his son's wife disappeared like three fleas off the end of a dog's tail. Ever hear tell about it?"

"Yes," said Mr. Grimble, his attention fairly caught at last. "Of course I heard of it. Nobody read anything else for a week. It came to be known as the great Van Suttart mystery. What about it?"

"Well," said Miad, his eyes narrowing, "there's this about it: There was a baby left behind called Cornelia Van Suttart. Mr. Frete brought her up in her own folks' house with no servants except his sister. He sent her to Barmingdale, and a week after she came back he asked her to marry him. When she wouldn't he tried something worse. Did you ever see the face of a man when he was all set to stop at nothing? I have. When a man is ready for murder or assault something funny happens to his face, see? Well, I helped Cornelia get out, and I've had reason to wonder ever since why Mr. Frete was so gol-durned anxious to keep her all for himself. Don't you wonder a bit, too, Mr. Grimble? Let me ring for a wet towel. Try wrapping it around your head."

There was a long silence, during which Mr. Grimble's shoulders gradually straightened and his vacant eyes grew bright and purposeful. In other words, he came to life, and when Mr. Grimble was himself he was very much of a man.

"Miad, " he said finally, "I'd like to see the girl. Do you think you could get her to come here?"

BEYOND REACH OF THE LAW

"I dunno," said Miad. "She's married now and perhaps her husband wouldn't like her to come to a place like this, but I'll try. When do you think would be a good time?"

"The sooner the better," said Mr. Grimble promptly. "If there's anything in what you've started me to thinking, you're right I'll want you for a partner. You have a way of putting things, Miad. Run along. Let me think my head off my neck while you fetch the girl."

At four o'clock that afternoon Miad ushered Cornelia into Mr. Grimble's presence with a great deal of pride. What was there to feel proud about? Naturally three years of penury and babies had turned Cornelia into a dull-eyed slattern. Wrong. Guess again. Look at her. Did you ever see anything lovelier in your life? Cheaply dressed in black—yes; but trim as a trysail. Slim and supple as a white birch, deep-bosomed, steady-eyed and with such a free sweep of the limb, and such a throbbing glow of health and courage as mark only the thoroughbred facing undaunted the five-bar hurdles of life, carrying every weight but money.

See the three of them sitting there—Lawyer Grimble behind his big flat desk, staring at Cornelia, drinking her in with the abject wistful admiration of middle age in the presence of triumphant youth and beauty; Miad on the edge of his seat, leaning forward, smiling quizzically; Cornelia sitting back at ease in her chair, her slim hands upon its arms, her knees close together and her eyes of Irish blue shining in understanding answer to Miad's smile, and turning to regard Mr. Grimble gravely whenever he spoke.

"But can't you remember anything?" asked Mr. Grimble of Cornelia after many other questions. "Of course you can't. You were a baby—a baby in arms. If only you could remember something. Something said or done, even by the Fretes, way back when they thought you were too young to understand."

"Wait," said Cornelia, throwing up her head. "I do. I do remember something."

She stopped speaking, the frown cleared from her brow and suddenly a surprised look spread over her face, her eyes crinkled at the corners and she laughed, low, musically, all to herself.

"Well," broke in Mr. Grimble impatiently, "what is it? What's the joke?"

Cornelia's face turned grave again, but the smile lingered in her eyes. "Not much," she said. "Only this: The cook, who must have died when I was about three years old, used to try to tell me something. All I can remember is that she used to say over and over again, 'Believe me, my lone darling, your dear mother would never have left her baby of her own free will.'"

"You're right; it's not much," said Mr. Grimble, frowning, "but it's something. At least it's in line. Why the laughter, by the way?"

"Don't you see?" said Cornelia, smiling outright again. "She called me a lone darling, and up to three minutes ago I always thought

she meant a loaned darling, a baby left in pawn
—a loan."

"Ha, ha!" laughed Mr. Grimble. "That *is*
funny."

"What's so funny about it?" demanded
Miad. "She was a baby, wasn't she? And she
learned what loan meant a durned sight
sooner than the other. What I'm thinking
about is that what that cook said was right.
What you going to do about it?"

"The first thing I'm going to do is to look
up all the known history of the firm that now
calls itself Van Suttart & Co.," said Mr. Grimble. "The way I'm going to do it is by inspect-
ing all public documents available—transfers
of property, mortgage payments and clear-
ances, and the change in the firm's name. If
I can find anything crooked I shall call for an
investigation of the books; but in the meantime
I need one thing—an unlimited power of attorney from Miss Van Suttart."

"She ain't Miss Van Suttart," interrupted
Miad. "I told you she was married."

BEYOND REACH OF THE LAW

"In that case," said Mr. Grimble, "the husband had better assign, too, but on a separate
form. What is your name now, my dear?"

Those words, "my" and "dear," were strictly unprofessional. They had slipped out on
their own account, simply because no honest
man of Mr. Grimble's age and natural courage
could look at Cornelia's pulsing loveliness
without automatically going the full limit of
permissible verbal license. Many a time when
the observing male does not dare take a liberty
with his itching fingers he does it with words.
Miad took no notice of the term of endear-
ment, nor did Cornelia, but when she drew a
long breath and answered, "My name is Grimble, the same as yours," and Mr. Grimble
merely grunted, "Indeed?" as he proceeded to
write out for his secretary the full name, Cornelia Van Suttart Grimble—why, then, they
did take notice.

Miad stared at Cornelia and Cornelia at
Miad with twin looks of chagrin that would
have been comical to a bystander but that to

themselves were tragic. Cornelia had exploded a bomb and, as far as Mr. Grimble was concerned, it had not made a sound. In ten minutes the standard form of absolute power of attorney had been filled out. Cornelia signed it with a hand that trembled a little, then arose and took two steps toward the door.

When Mr. Grimble asked her if she could not spare him a few moments more she turned, regarded him gravely and said quite clearly, "No, Mr. Grimble. It's high time I got back to your grandchildren."

"Grandchildren!" exclaimed Mr. Grimble. "Grandchildren!" At the repetition he rose from his seat as slowly and majestically as a balloon taking to the air. "Did you say my ——"

He gulped twice and then exploded. "Harold! You're Mrs. Harold Grimble! The young fool! The wooden-headed Indian! Nincompoop! Why didn't he tell me? Confound his bullheaded impudence! Why couldn't he——"

BEYOND REACH OF THE LAW

"Stop!" cried Cornelia, whirling to face, with blazing eyes, her empurpled father-in-law. "Don't you dare say another word against Harold. You were the wooden-headed Indian! You were! You were! He tried to tell you, but you wouldn't let him. And bullheaded too! I'll say it! I'll call you everything you called him. I—I hate you!"

"My dear, dear girl," gasped Mr. Grimble, stepping around to get between Cornelia and the door. "Please! Please forgive me! You are right—dead right. I'll call myself all those names over and over again, if you'll only give me one chance to see my grandchildren and Harold—a life-long chance, I mean. I can't imagine how it happened, my not letting him tell me. You see, my dear, when you think a boy has just stepped around the corner for lunch and he comes back married— why, you simply can't listen to anything about the girl or anything else. Don't you see? You just can't."

"It wasn't lunch," gulped Cornelia, dabbing

at her eyes with just such a pocket handkerchief as the one with which she had once wiped out of Miad's eight-year-old ear the blood Harold Grimble had caused to flow. "It—it was dinner."

"So it was," agreed Mr. Grimble hastily, "and he stayed out all night. I was a fool— a wooden-headed, bullheaded fool. A—a nincompoop."

"Oh, no, you weren't," said Cornelia with a quick reversal, and smiling at him over the handkerchief, still at work on her nose and cheeks, "Not really. You just couldn't see how a nice girl could have been the one to do a thing like that. But it had to be Mr. Crabbe or Miad or Harold, and I chose Harold."

"Thank God!" exclaimed Mr. Grimble.

"Say," broke in Miad, jolting Mr. Grimble's elbow, "how's the wooden head? Does it begin to see why Mr. Prosper Frete is after you?"

This chronicle has nothing to say about the reunion of the Grimbles, father, mother, son and grandchildren; it is concerned strictly with a litigation unique in the annals of the New York courts, a case still remembered by the legal profession and a few others as the Van Suttart Succession versus Prosper Frete *et al.* Nothing short of the cataclysmic disturbances consequent upon a great civil war would have permitted the laying of the foundations for such a barefaced and gigantic fraud.

Go back in your own mind or somebody else's to the decade between 1863 and the financial panic of 1873. Remember that strange readjustments, irregular at any other time, were made during those years. Many a man had died, leaving his business and property in a tangle. Many another had merely disappeared, making things still more difficult for partners and heirs. Many had turned up, as did William Van Suttart, from the dead, demanding readjustments of readjustments, and so on, *ad infinitum.* Then, heaped on top of it all, came the most disastrous panic in the history of the nation. More readjustments.

GREAT VAN SUTTART MYSTERY

In addition to all those things, remember that Mr. Frete was a partner, though a junior, of the ancient Van Suttart establishment, with power to sign, seal, receive and deliver. Recollect further that he had the foresight of a vulture and the cunning premonition of a weasel waiting for a hen to lay an egg. Figure out for yourself how easy and how natural it would be for such a man, suddenly confronted with the disappearance of his business associates, to withdraw all the loose collateral and cash of the firm and put it in a safe place under his sole responsibility pending the reappearance of the rightful owners.

From that point watch him with his sister take immediate charge of the Van Suttart house and the abandoned baby for a day, a month, a year, a decade. At first, puzzlement as to what had really become of the Van Suttarts, then conviction that they were indeed gone, never to return. Acceptance of the fact with pious gratitude to whatever twisted deity Mr. Frete was wont to render thanks. Skillful doctoring of the books and endless juggling of stocks and titles. Years of covering up tracks in a time when tracks were easily covered. The conception of the idea of marriage, reaching its tentacles forward to the baby's womanhood. Calculation. The birth of an immutable policy, the pale eye of the male Frete saying to the pale eye of the female Frete, "All is well; all will be well. Silence, for I know what you are thinking. Silence, and let the mills of the gods grind for us."

It can be seen that it would be no part of Mr. Frete's scheme to go through the process necessary to marrying an orphaned minor with no legal guardian. Such a move would have entailed the raising of exactly the questions for which he had no answer. Consequently he had to wait until she had attained her majority.

By the time Cornelia was turned eighteen he had entrenched himself within a formidable paper fortress. Inside the fortress was a labyrinth and within the labyrinth a maze. At the dead center of the maze was Mr. Prosper

Frete, but even so, he knew that only marriage with Cornelia would consolidate his position beyond possibility of conquest, beyond attack, beyond even a flutter of anxiety.

Cleverly cheated out of marrying her, he did not give up the fort. By no means. He merely intensified its defenses and ended finally by overreaching himself. His very shrewdness betrayed him. When he strove to rip every trace of the sinews of war from anyone who by any chance might fight for Cornelia's rights, he ended by arousing the suspicions of a born explorer in the realms of motive. His scheme would have been the exact right thing with numskulls or even directed against average intelligence, but Miad Blake, pugnacious almost from the day of his birth, was anything but a numskull. In battle he might be as direct as a cannon ball, but when penetrating the minds of crooked men he was as devious and persistent as a maggot.

The investigation instituted by Mr. Grimble brought to light by deduction a great many black marks against Mr. Frete, one added laboriously to another—but by deduction only. Mr. Frete did not crumble; he did not even wince. He stood on a single rock, apparently indifferent to and unmoved by the waves of eloquence of counsel for the Van Suttart Succession, Plaintiff. The rock was comprised in a single statement not over ten lines long. It was as follows: The defense contended that the three Van Suttarts had not disappeared within the meaning of the law; they had absconded, taking with them every available security and all the cash of the firm of which defendant was an integral member through partnership. Proof lay in the fact that in the course of time all the securities had come upon the market in widely separated cities, and even from abroad.

That was the rock. The seaweed trimmings ran into sixty foolscap pages, which set forth the great struggle of defendant to save the ancient name of Van Suttart from bankruptcy and shame; the long years of goodness of defendant toward the waif who was principal plaintiff; the money spent on said waif and her education out of the pocket of defendant; finally her astonishing ingratitude and alliance with self-seeking bloodsuckers. Would the Court please take the books of Van Suttart & Co.; examine them, and let them speak for the defendant. The reorganization from nothing was his. The profits were his. The plaintiff really owed Mr. Prosper Frete, her benefactor, a lot of money.

Against these walls counsel for the Van Suttart Succession sounded its trumpet, at first with faith that they would certainly fall. Why in eighteen years had there never been a transfer of Van Suttart real property by sale, in spite of advantageous offers? Was defendant afraid of the title searcher? Why had defendant lived so secluded a life, making a drudge of his sister even after he had attained to affluence? Was every contact of his own household with the outer world a danger? Why had he sued so ardently for the hand of Cornelia Van Suttart? What stake was large enough to make him forget that assault was a penitentiary offense? Why had he not dared act before she was of age? Was he afraid lest he bring tumbling about his head a fraudulent fabrication through the reflex action of the laws for the protection of minors? Was it not true that the fortune at stake greatly exceeded the million mark? Did defendant seriously contend that he had started with nothing on the day of the disappearance of the Van Suttarts?

In the face of such libelous accusations counsel for the defense merely smiled, licked its chops and murmured, "To abscond is not to disappear in the meaning of the law."

Against that rock Mr. Grimble hurled himself at first valiantly, then desperately and finally despairingly. He bought a file of all the daily papers covering the great Van Suttart mystery and read the blurred print through and through until his eye-balls burned in their sockets. He called in Miad and made him read the baffling story from end to end, over and over again, every version, every supposition, every deduction. Not every clew; for there was no clew. Not one. Absolute mystery. A blank wall. No toe hold. Not a crevice. To make matters worse, Miad's twelve-hundred-dollar fighting fund was rapidly melting away and, to his shame, Mr. Grimble knew not how to replenish it.

"God help us, Miad!" he groaned late one night, holding his aching head in both hands. "If we don't find out what became of the three Van Suttarts—why, we're lost."

"Lost!" gasped Miad. "What are you saying? Don't you know he done all you said? Didn't everybody know it in their bones?"

"Corpus delicti," moaned Mr. Grimble, more to himself than in answer. *"Corpus delicti."*

"What the hell?" asked Miad. "Hey! Wake up. What you saying?"

"Corpus delicti," repeated Mr. Grimble.

"It means the essential fact in the commission of a crime—the actual body in the murder."

Miad's belligerent eyes protruded. "Say," he said, "you're getting worse and worse. I ain't the judge. You tell me plain what you mean."

"Just this," said Mr. Grimble, coming to himself and giving Miad stare for stare: "If we can't find those three bodies—dead, mind you, dead these twenty years—why, our case is done for, finished, lost. That's what I mean."

"You big fool," murmured Miad, "didn't all them news hounds try to find out and fail? Didn't all the cops and detectives have a go right when it happened, and never got a smell? You stay up tonight and think of something else. I'm going."

CHAPTER XVI

BURIED THESE TWENTY YEARS

AFTER this disturbing interview Miad could not work, nor could he stay peacefully in Cobbled Court. He walked and walked, ranging from river to river and from Battery to Central Park. He would look questioningly at passers-by, at the pavement, at the walls of houses, at ferry-boats, at street cars and at the fat-horsed Fifth Avenue busses. All in vain. Nothing—no one—could tell him what would become of Cornelia and her two babies if the Van Suttart Succession went down in defeat beneath the Juggernaut of Prosper Frete's machination.

As for Harold, Harold was a man. As for Crabbe—why, Crabbe was rapidly shrinking to nothing at all. Only yesterday he had cackled: "You won't have to embalm me, Miad. Not much. All you got to do along of me, Miad, will be to leave me lay on the roof for half an hour and get sun cured. Yes, sir. Tough as horsehide. Hang me on a hook anywhere instead of burying. Cheaper than anything anybody else ever thought on. That's Crabbe, Miad; your old man Crabbe. Nobody else ever thought on it." As for himself, Miad cared nothing at all. But Cornelia? Why, Cornelia was Cornelia! He couldn't let anything happen to Cornelia, he just couldn't.

Thinking these thoughts his troubled eyes fell on the pillar of flesh once familiar to every habitué of upper Fifth Avenue as the stupendous doorman at Borlay's. The pillar's name was Patrick O'Dowd, and he was a landmark not so much by reason of his great size or advanced age or of his looks, which were terrible, or of his courtesy, strictly negative even to Borlay's best and oldest customers, but because he had never been known to unbend or to smile. Suddenly Miad became professional. What a chance for a small stroke of business! Why had he never thought of it before? Gee, what a skeleton!

The day was unseasonably cold and O'Dowd was standing within the sparse shelter of the stately portico which it was his duty to decorate and guard. Presently an individual whom he could not see without bending, and consequently did not see, approached him and said in a perky voice at about the level of O'Dowd's belt, "Got a match, Cap?"

O'Dowd could hardly believe his ears. Who dared thus to speak to him while he was on duty, incased in grandeur and his brass-bound uniform? A convulsive tremor quivered up and down through his enormous frame, shaking the pedestal of a supernal complacence. The invisible antennæ possessed by all pompous dignity told him that the diminutive owner of the perky voice was actually waiting. There were no pockets in O'Dowd's unwrinkled frock coat. He lifted one of its skirts, thrust a hand into his trouser's pocket, fished out a box of matches, held it out, dropped it.

"Keep them," he rumbled, his basilisk stare never wavering from the horizontal.

On the following day at precisely the same hour the same perky voice said to Mr. O'Dowd, "Say, Cap, got a match?"

O'Dowd did not shake this time; he trembled with rage. Rather than demean himself by a fracas with a runt, he hastened to comply. He surrendered a second box of matches, which, by the way, were not given away in that day with every five-cent cigar. For several moments thereafter he stood in a dumb daze and then a thought struck him, an Irish thought of the little people and their pranks.

Or worse—it might be something worse— He shot a lightning glance to right and left, up and down the street. Too late. Why hadn't he looked at the stranger in time? How did he know there was any stranger? What if the perky voice had come alone without anyone with it? Who but a banshee would dare twice so to address Patrick T. H. O'Dowd? He looked down with horrid premonition, and his snow-white hair rose within the wide bell of his smart blue cap. At his feet on the door-mat lay the packet of matches.

On the next afternoon at precisely the same time, before the perky voice could get further than "Say, Cap—" O'Dowd's two hands shot forward, and to his surprise and vast relief came to grips with a real, honest-to-goodness human throat. He tightened his fingers and lifted his tormentor almost clear of the pave-ment. Then did Patrick, the pillar, forget himself and the reputation it had taken years to build. He unbent, became molten and pres-ently began to flow as follows: "Say who do youse take me for, you half as big as a minute! The Ruby Match Company? You get out of here or I'll call the dog catcher, and don't you ever come back. See? Now, git!"

O'Dowd did not look into space as he spoke these words, but straight down into the snapping slate-blue eyes of a compact individual who was not so very undersized, taken as a whole, except as anyone is undersized when standing in the shadow of the Metropolitan Tower.

"Just as well you let me go when you did, you big stiff," growled Miad as soon as released, "or I'd of kicked off both your knee-caps. I didn't want your old matches. All I wanted was for you to lean over the edge of the roof and talk to me. How would we of looked with me putting a step-ladder up against you? But that's what I would of brought next time—a stepladder."

"You stepladder yourself around the block —" began O'Dowd, and stopped.

Have you ever amused yourself by staring fixedly at a stranger's feet and watching for results? Miad was not staring at O'Dowd's feet, he was doing less and worse. He was staring at the geographical center of the broad expanse of O'Dowd's pillarlike torso. So intent and avid was his gaze that the huge man ceased speaking and with a vapid look passed one hand anxiously down over his creaseless front.

"What are you looking at?" he asked surlily.

"You," replied Miad without shifting his solemn gaze.

"What's the matter of me?" asked O'Dowd nervously. "What do you want anyway?"

"What do I want?" echoed Miad imperturbably. "I'll tell you what I want. I want something you got, and that when I want it you won't need it any more. I want it so bad that when you fix it so I can have it, I'll give you fifty bucks; and when I get it I'll give your widow fifty more."

"My widow!" exploded O'Dowd. "Did you say my widow?"

"Sure," replied Miad. "Let's be reasonable. You ain't got long to live. Don't you want to talk business while you can?"

"No," grunted O'Dowd. "No, I don't. No."

BURIED THESE TWENTY YEARS

"All right," said Miad calmly; "then I'll wait."

"Wait?" gasped O'Dowd. "What for? You don't think—" Once more a Goliath fell before a David. "Oh, well, I'll come with you if it's only to get shut of you. Do your waiting around the corner. It's past time for closing here and I'll be with you as soon as ever I shed me uniform."

When he reappeared a quarter of an hour later in mufti no one would have known him for the day-long watchdog of the stately portal. Incased and held in place by reënforced broadcloth and gold braid, he was straight as a ramrod and did not look his age by ten years. But in his home clothes anyone could see that he was an old man, though well preserved through long pickling in the wind of all weathers. Miad, walking beside the slouching giant, felt a vague disappointment. Would the skeleton prove really the magnificent specimen he had coveted so ardently? He cocked a knowing eye at O'Dowd and was immediately reassured. If the splendid frame still retained a full set of teeth it would be a prize of the very first water. Unfortunately a low-drooping, thick-bodied mustache prevented his seeing the big man's mouth, let alone his teeth.

The two left Fifth Avenue by one accord and walked westward. Arriving at Sixth, they turned south and presently entered a spacious establishment where each table looked like an oasis in a desert of imitation Carrara marble and the odors of garlic and spaghetti waged unequal yet interminable war. They picked a far corner and sat down. O'Dowd fixed Miad with a baleful eye.

"Now, you," he began, "what made you say I ain't got long to live? What makes you think I got a widow—a widow to have, I mean? And what in thunder do you want anyway?"

"Not so fast," said Miad coolly. "I want to see you eat first. If you can't chew tough meat the deal is off, see? Your teeth is probably rotten."

BURIED THESE TWENTY YEARS

"My teeth rotten!" cried O'Dowd, his eyes glaring. "Rotten, is they? Take a look."

He lifted his mustache with a giant index finger and opened an enormous mouth, a cavernous mouth, a vast pink shell of a mouth, equipped with a veritable stockade of perfect yellow teeth. Miad stared, quivered and sank back in his chair. His eyes grew glassy with the intensity of his gaze. Yet he was not looking at O'Dowd's tremendous mouth nor at his teeth. He was looking at his lip—his lower lip—which was deeply indented by a most peculiarly shaped scar.

"Who are you?" he murmured, low, but so intensely that the giant snapped his jaws shut and cast a quick glance over his shoulder before answering.

"Patrick O'Dowd," he murmured back, leaning forward. "Not at your service. Now, what's *your* name?"

"Miad," said Miad with a very unusual tremor in his voice; "Miad Blake."

The effect was electrical. The giant's face

raced through one quick change in expression to another until it had covered the entire gamut from vacuous wonder to welcoming joy.

"Miad, me lad!" he cried, reaching over to grasp both of Miad's shoulders and shake them affectionately. "There's only the one Miad in all the world. Sure, boy, I'm a blockhead, for ye ain't changed since you was three years old. Same bug eyes lookin' for a fight, same hair, same size all but an inch or two. Do ye mind the times you rode me neck, lad? Do ye remember biting a small steak out of me lower lip? Ha, ha! Haw, haw! I'll bet your little behind is flat yet from the wallop I give it!"

They sat, they talked, they ate, they reminisced. Miad explained that he had been attracted by O'Dowd's magnificent physique and had wished to get an option on such a splendid specimen of a skeleton. The way he talked about it made O'Dowd feel important, handsome and generous. He said Miad could have the skeleton for nothing as soon as he himself was through with it. There was no longer any Lady O'Dowd, consequently there would be no widow. Speaking of women, but and by the way——

"Miad, do ye remember why it was ye bit me?"

"Sure," said Miad. "You asked me did my daddy used to call my mother Mary, and then I bit you. I don't know why."

The big man nodded his massive head, pushed away his plate and leaned forward. "That was the way of it," he said. "Son, you guessed I didn't mean no good, and you guessed right, so you bit me. But them days is far away now. Let me tell you, quiet-like. Your father was John Blake, porter around to Van Suttart's. When he quit I got his job, see? I'm big, but I ain't anybody's fool. I seen things, queer things; one all-fired mortal queer thing. I thought it out. I did that, and got no spick of money for my pains. All of a sudden something happened and it was too late. Do you want I should tell you the mortal queer thing?"

Miad was very intent. He sat on the edge of his chair with both heels caught in the front rung and leaned forward, elbows on the table, chin in hands.

"Go ahead," he said. "I ain't going to bite you again, whatever you say."

"Well, it's this here," continued O'Dowd gravely. "Your mother, Mary Malone Blake, as true a woman as ever stepped, and Mrs. William Van Suttart was one and the same body."

Miad did not cry out. He sat outwardly perfectly still, but the blood within his veins and pulses raced and leaped with an overwhelming fury. To make matters worse, a huge lump sprang into his throat and stayed there. Think! He wanted to think. God give him air! Mary Malone Blake. Mrs. William Van Suttart. One and the same. His mother, as true a woman as ever stepped, was Mrs. William Van Suttart. But Mrs. Van

BURIED THESE TWENTY YEARS

Suttart was Cornelia's mother. Why—Cornelia! Oh! Oh! Cornelia! He scrambled to his feet, reeled, caught the table, steadied himself.

"Come with me, O'Dowd, will you?" he begged. "I got to go somewheres. I got to go now, and you got to come."

Ten minutes later they had boarded the Sixth Avenue Elevated and O'Dowd was bending forward to mask Miad's face from the sight of curious strangers. Within himself, Miad had returned to childhood in every sense of the word. He was caught in his mother's arms for that last tight embrace. He was fighting for Cornelia, playing with Cornelia, bossing Cornelia. His eyes stared and stared, far away, far back. His fingers picked at his corduroy trousers. Spaced tears, one at a time, far apart, crawled unheeded down his cheeks. They arrived at a little house in Waverly Place. Miad found the door on the latch, opened it and entered, followed by the wondering O'Dowd.

"Who is that?" called Cornelia in a voice whose mere inflection told of sleeping babies.

"It's me—Miad," gulped Miad over the lump in his throat.

He did not see Harold, reading a book behind the big table lamp; he saw only Cornelia as she sat in a sway-backed chair, her knees draped with little stockings, her fingers busy, high lights in her glossy hair and two home fires burning steadily in her deep blue eyes as she raised them to cast Miad a swift warm look of welcome and kept them raised to stare, troubled, at the astounding bulk of the stranger, Patrick O'Dowd.

"What is it, Miad? What has happened?"

Suddenly Miad's compact frame seemed to crumple. He hurled himself forward, fell on his knees, dropped his face in Cornelia's lap and burst into a paroxysm of sobs. She threw her arms about him and drew his head against her breast.

"Miad!" she cried, full throated, and then more softly: "Oh, Miad, my dear, dear boy,

what is the matter? What has happened? Tell
Cornelia. Tell Corny." Miad's hands groped
around her body and clung to her. They were
strangely like the hands of a baby.

"You're my sister," he wailed at last. "My
own sister. And I'm dirty and common and
poor. I'm only Miad Blake."

For an instant Cornelia sat rigid; then she
looked up at the vast stranger. She did not
have to speak. Not with those eyes. Not
after that look. As Harold rose, wondering,
to his feet O'Dowd stepped forward, twirling his hat nervously between his huge
hands.

"It's true, miss. I was porter at Van Suttart's when you was born. Your mother was
married to Miad's father when she thought
young Mr. Van Suttart was long dead in the
war. Mary Malone Van Suttart; then Mary
Malone Blake through no fault of her own,
poor dear; and then Mrs. William Van Suttart again for the honor she bore to God, Him
rest her soul! And Miad left behind in Cob-

bled Court. Two years old or there-abouts he
must of been when you come, miss, and I know
it all through watching of her go to see him
before the sorry day the banshees swept them
all away, her and William and old Skinflint
Van Suttart—pardon the word, miss."

"Cornelia," said Miad, striving to draw out
of her rigid arms, "no one has got to know,
only us four. No one. Not even the children,
if you don't want 'em to. No one else, Corny.
Only us four."

"Miad! Do you think I'm ashamed— Oh,
Miad!"

Cornelia's shoulders suddenly slumped.
Her fingers crooked and dug deep into Miad's
back. Her eyelids closed tightly. Her lips
began to twitch.

"Harold," she whispered, "go. Go out.
Take the man. Close the door. Quickly."
And then a sound as of the mother of all love,
crooning, sobbing, crooning again.

"Miad! Dear Miad. My own sweet
brother. Oh! Oh! Oh! Miad, my darling.

Always. Always in my heart. Always! Oh!
—oh!—oh!"

Draw the curtain, Harold. Quick; close
the door. Tightly. Shut yourself away from
that sound, for it is not yours to hear, nor
mine, nor anyone's save Miad Blake's. Yesterday the lone son of the city of New York;
today Cornelia's brother! Talk it over in the
hall with Patrick O'Dowd. Let in your
father, with trouble heavy on his brow. Tell
it to him too. Whisper, all three of you.
Stand around. Wait. Give Mr. Grimble a
chance to pump O'Dowd, porter at Van Suttart's at the very time of the great Van
Suttart mystery. But hold on. Hark. Cornelia is calling you in. They enter and find
Miad looking not at all sheepish over his recent
tears. His face is plain out-and-out happy.
It is all aglow, as if it had been scrubbed with
some heavenly-angel brand of soap.

He turned eagerly as the three men entered.
"Tell her, O'Dowd. Tell her again, everything, how it happened. She wants to know.

She's glad. She's glad I'm her own half brother."

O'Dowd sat on the sofa, for there was no chair big enough to hold him, and began to repeat his thrice-told tale with a wealth of detail and corroborative evidence which made those who had already heard it perk up their ears. The old man forgot the pride of his present condition as the landmark at Borlay's. He closed his eyes and deliberately moved himself back to the days before the war. It seemed it must be long since he had had anyone who wished to hear him talk, he was so chockablock with words. He drew a picture; made them see it. Another; yet another. He showed them sweet Mary Malone and the tortured world in which she moved.

Ah, yes. Every day. Every day she would come to the office for a quiet word with William Van Suttart and presently go away fleetly, never twice in succession in the same direction. O'Dowd, out on an errand, had just chanced on a glimpse of her turning into Cobbled Court. He thought naught of it. Months passed. Then he chanced to see her again passing swiftly down the short narrow gullet of Hague Street, turning into Cobbled Court. From then on it had been easy for him to add bit to bit. When——

A loud cry crashed across the rumble of O'Dowd's voice. Miad was on his feet, staring, eyes wide open, mouth wide open, gulping, gagging. Cornelia's babies awoke and began to murmur querulously. She went to them. O'Dowd, Mr. Grimble and Harold cast startled looks at Miad. The lawyer was the first to recover.

"Well?" he asked. "What has come over you?"

"My mother!" gasped Miad. "Cornelia's mother. Holding me tight, the last time—the very last time I seen her. 'Oh, baby, my dear, dear boy,' she said, 'why did you run from your mother?' That's what she said."

"Well, what about it?" prompted Mr. Grimble.

GREAT VAN SUTTART MYSTERY

"You don't understand," said Miad. "You don't see it like I do. There's three rooms under Hague Street now; there used to be two more before they finished cleaning up alongside of the bridge. The day she chased me through the tunnel from Cobbled Court, that last time I ever seen her, the wester'most room was fallen in, and the one next to it, the one where she caught me, had a hole in the roof. One minute you could look up and see the great wall of Brooklyn Bridge, and the next minute you couldn't, because two men was a-shutting out of the light. One of 'em said very loud perhaps the finger of God made that hole. My mother turned whiter than white. She looked up and cried out 'William!' like something had caught her by the throat— like she was choking to death. Then some earth come sliding down and she said, 'Run, darling! Run!' and give me a push. I run. I run because she told me to, but mostly on account of the loudest, dullest noise I ever heard, just behind me, chasing me."

BURIED THESE TWENTY YEARS

"Wait a minute, Miad," interrupted Mr. Grimble, whose face had grown exceedingly tense. "Let's get this straight as we go along. What was the noise like?"

Miad turned from gazing fixedly at nothing to look Mr. Grimble straight in the eyes.

"It sounded heavy," he said, "like stones, mortar and dirt a-falling, and the reason it sounded like that is because that is what it was. I never seen my mother again; nobody never seen the Van Suttarts again. That's where they be today—all three on 'em—under the yard of the Hague Street house, buried these twenty years."

"If that is so," said Mr. Grimble very quietly—"and I believe it is so—then our troubles are over and Prosper Frete will go to jail tomorrow."

"You can bet your last dollar it's so," said Miad assuredly. "It was lunch time they disappeared, according to the papers. The men that was filling in all the holes along the bridge was probably off having their beer, comfortable. But seeings is believing. All we got to do is to get busy tonight and dig away the rubble."

Mr. Grimble had expected to enter the court room on the following morning with the feelings of a convicted murderer crossing the threshold of the death house, for defeat in the case against Prosper Frete meant more than failure; it spelled utter ruin. As it was, and to the amazement of counsel for the defense, he walked in with head held high and shoulders squared. No sooner was the court called to order than he addressed the bench.

"Your Honor, I move for permission to reopen this case, as I am in possession of new evidence of crucial importance. I beg to announce to the court and to opposing counsel that the great Van Suttart mystery is no longer a mystery. The exact hour of the death of the three missing Van Suttarts—namely, at noon on the day of their disappearance—has been specifically established, as will be proved. Your Honor, the bodies of the elder

BURIED THESE TWENTY YEARS

Van Suttart, of his son William, and of Mary Malone Van Suttart, have been found."

When Mr. Prosper Frete heard those words his face and his hands, placed on the back of the seat in front of him, turned to a yellowish green and he began to tremble with minute vibrations. He was palsied with terror. His pale eyes alone remained active and darted despairing glances this way and that, as though imploring his stricken body to leap, dart, dodge and follow. Then they were met, checked and held by Miad Blake's steel-gray gaze. The effect was as though Mr. Frete had been manacled at that instant instead of several days later when sentence of imprisonment for twenty years was pronounced.

Why go into the details of the restitution of the Van Suttart fortune or the reorganization of Van Suttart & Co., once Hendricks, Jacob Hendricks, Van Suttart and Partners, into plain Grimble, Blake & Co.? Why describe the successful apotheosis of old man Crabbe via the sun-dried route or the burgeoning of new buds on the Grimble family tree? Why indeed, since happiness has no history? Let us hop, skip and jump, instead, to a sunny afternoon in May of 1920. Behold Miad, fifty years old, sitting beside his hat on a bench in the park with both legs extended. Changed? Not a bit of it. Look at him; look hard and you will see the shock-headed, fighting-eyed youngster who at the age of three stepped out to take life as he found it, by assault. On one of his chunky knees sits Corny's eldest's youngest; on the other, her youngest's eldest. Hear the latter speak.

"Uncle Miad, tell us the tack-come-at-us goldfish again. Please, Uncle Miad."

"The trachomatous goldfish, now," says Miad, his eyes growing round and staring. "Well, he was a queer bird of a fish, and no error. Believe me, he was. Did you ever see a leper with a long white beard? No? Never seen one, eh? Well, that was what he looked like. White spots. Long silky beard. How do you think he got caught, eh? Listen. I'll

tell you a big secret and don't you ever forget
it. He never would of got caught only he
didn't know how to keep his mouth shut.
See?"

Thus Miad to Cornelia's grandchildren on a
bench in the park—the same bench and the
same park where he told me this tale of not so
long ago.

THE END